BUSTED!

Also by Betty Hicks

Animal House and Iz
I Smell Like Ham

BUSTED!

BETTY HICKS

A DEBORAH BRODIE BOOK
ROARING BROOK PRESS
BROOKFIELD, CONNECTICUT

ACKNOWLEDGMENTS

I would like to express my gratitude to youth soccer coaches
Gary Anderson and Kenny Steed for reading my soccer scenes
to ensure their accuracy.

I would also like to thank my editor, Deborah Brodie, for her
wisdom, insight, and patience with the overextended
mother of the bride.

A Deborah Brodie Book

Published by Roaring Brook Press

A Division of Holtzbrinck Publishing Holdings Limited Partnership

2 Old New Milford Road, Brookfield, Connecticut 06804

Library of Congress Cataloging-in-Publication Data

Hicks, Betty.

Busted!/Betty Hicks.--1st ed.

p. cm.

"A Deborah Brodie Book."

Summary: Anxious to distract his "overly" strict mother, twelve-year-old Stuart and his best
friend, a girl named Mack, determine to fix her up with Mack's Uncle Joe.

[1. Mothers--Fiction. 2. Single-parent families--Fiction. 3. Behavior--Fiction. 4. Humorous
stories.] I. Title.

PZ7.H53155Bu 2004

[Fic]--dc22   2003017830

ISBN 1-59643-004-4

10   9   8   7   6   5   4   3   2   1

Book design by Jennifer Browne

Printed in the United States of America

First edition

FOR BILL

CONTENTS

1

MACK RULES!

Friday night. Nine thirty.

Stuart Ellis was grounded.

Stuck at home for the third time in three weeks. With all his computer privileges revoked.

He might as well be extinct.

Whoomp. He flopped onto his bed and stared at the ceiling, wishing he were at Robert's house, watching a rented movie. Or at We've Got Game, the video arcade.

He glanced at his computer and wished he could boot it up to work on his Web site, or maybe IM Mack.

Ha! As if Mackenzie Eller would be home on a Friday night. As if anyone would be home.

Stuart gazed longingly across the room at the video game cartridges scattered all across the top of his bookshelf—the ones he wasn't allowed to play anymore. Books lined the next shelf: *Jeremy Thatcher—Dragon Hatcher*, *Holes*, *The Book of Three*, and a handful of Matt Christopher soccer books, all propped up by a fat

rubber dragon that thrashed its tail if Stuart remembered to change its batteries.

Stuart had always loved dragons. He thought they
were pretty cool. Big scaly beasts, exhaling fire.

He could even make an awesome dragon shadow with
his hands, way better than those one-eyed dog heads that
anybody could do. A useless talent, thought Stuart, that
came from being grounded for life.

Which reminded him of the biggest dragon of all. His
mother. The same mom who had played Crazy Eights
and ridden bikes with him for eleven years. Then, *presto-
chango*, sometime after his twelfth birthday, when he
hadn't been paying attention, she'd turned into a fire-
breathing, spying, interfering, cold-blooded dragon.

Not that he wanted to play cards or ride bikes with
her anymore. He'd rather play video games and soccer.

Video games, Stuart thought miserably. No longer
allowed.

But by eleven o'clock, his mother would be asleep—
totally zonked after a whole day working as a shop man-
ager *and* a dragon. Then he could sneak downstairs and
turn on the Comedy Channel.

Hadn't Mom wanted him to expand his vocabulary?
Didn't late-night TV teach him tons of new words?

He sighed. He couldn't chance it. After all, that's what
had gotten him grounded in the first place.

Not that what he'd been watching had been so bad.
No. It had been funny. Some goofball big guy with weird

hair and no neck struggling around in a circle, pretending to be a dorky dad folding his kid's stroller and trying to catch a bus at the same time. Then, at the exact moment that Stuart's mom showed up, yawning and adjusting her bathrobe, the man began to curse the stroller. Cuss words that Stuart knew, and some that he didn't. Words bad enough to make a guy's gut twist if his mother appeared.

And she always did.

Stuart didn't understand how he could watch TV for hours and not see or hear anything more PG-13 than *Men in Black* blasting space bugs. Then, out of nowhere, cuss words. Or worse—some girl wearing a supertight dress, grabbing the main guy and kissing his face off. For no reason at all. That's when Stuart's mom *always* came strolling through the den, reminding him to take out the trash or start his homework.

It never failed.

His friend Mack had an explanation. She called it the Telepathic Parent Principle. And it applied to plenty of things besides TV—like forgotten chores, bad grades, or so much as *thinking* about sneaking out. It was that weird talent that parents had of seeing trouble before you even got into it.

Mack had another theory, too—one that explained why Stuart's mother had turned into a dragon about the same time he turned twelve.

"Preteen proclivities," she quoted from one of her

ten jillion magazines, "can produce single-parent panic."

"Huh?" Stuart had said.

"The normal stuff you're into now," Mack explained, tossing the article aside. "You know—puberty. It scares your mom. Especially since you don't have a dad to help her deal."

Mack was a year older than Stuart and ten times smarter. She had everything totally figured out, even the first time they'd met.

It was spring, three years ago. Stuart and his mom had lived at 401 Peach Street only a week. Stuart was dragging empty moving boxes from his new house out to the curb when Mack marched up his front walk, swinging her skinny arms and wearing a T-shirt—with pajama bottoms!

At least Stuart assumed they were pajama bottoms. After all, they were loose and baggy and sky blue, with fluffy white clouds floating all over them.

"Mail," she announced, thrusting a white envelope toward him.

Even back then, when Mack was only ten, and Stuart nine, Mack ruled. Not in a bad way. But she did have this major, kick-butt confidence pumping out of her. Everything Stuart *didn't* have.

"Huh?" said Stuart.

"Are you Jamie Ellis?" Mack flapped the extended

envelope up and down in front of him. She flashed a superfriendly smile. "I'm Mackenzie Eller. Call me Mack."

"I'm Stuart," he croaked, trying to make his voice sound deep. It wasn't a flirting thing. He didn't even like girls. But something about Mack had made him want to be older than nine. He heaved an empty box onto the curb, hoping to make it look as if it contained concrete.

"Jamie Ellis is my mother," he explained.

"Oh," said Mack, blinking her eyes four times in a row. Stuart learned later that when she blinked like that—fast and focused—it meant she was thinking. Which could be a good thing or a bad thing.

"My dad's name is James Eller," she said, pointing at a yellow frame house across the street and five doors down. "That's our house. 410 Peach Street. Not 401." She pointed at the number on Stuart's mailbox, then flipped her straight red hair back from her face. "We got your mail."

"Weird," said Stuart, staring at Mack's house and trying to sort out the wacky name and address thing. He saw a two-story house with lots of trees and a garage at the end of the driveway. A soccer goal, one swing, two scooters, and three bikes crowded the front yard. How many kids lived there, anyway?

Stuart thought some more about the name coincidence. How nutty that his mom and the father of this person wearing pajama bottoms had the same name.

Well, almost the same. James Eller. Jamie Ellis. So close. What if James Eller married his mom? Wouldn't they practically be the same person?

Every now and then, Stuart found himself wondering if his mother would marry again. He hoped not. The rest of the time he concentrated on playing soccer and mastering video games.

"Longer," said Mack, tilting her head.

"Huh?"

"You'd look cool with longer hair."

Stuart reached up and touched his thick, curly hair. Was this girl wacko? What kind of lamebrain went around telling people they didn't even know how to cut their hair?

Mackenzie Eller. That's who.

Stuart's life hadn't been the same since.

2

WHAT'S A GUY TO DO?

Saturday morning. Eight fifty-five. Stuart rang Mack's doorbell. Three times.

He waited. He jogged in place. It was cold.

Eventually, Mrs. Eller opened the door. She was a big, round woman, not quite fat, but hefty—like she could lift a car if she needed to. She pushed her red, frizzy, sleep-tangled hair back with one hand and pulled her bathrobe closed with the other. The robe had a coffee stain on the sleeve that looked just like a spider.

"Stuart," she said, eyeing his shin guards and soccer cleats. "Are you lost?"

"No ma'am. I'm on my way to soccer practice. Has Mack left for her piano lesson yet?"

"Mack has piano today?" asked Mrs. Eller, puzzled. Sometimes Mrs. Eller seemed to forget that she even had children.

"Oh, yes," she remembered suddenly. "At ten o'clock. Or is it twelve?"

"She awake yet?" asked Stuart.

"I seriously doubt it," laughed Mrs. Eller. She turned and hurried toward the kitchen as smells of burning bacon drifted past Stuart's nose.

Mrs. Eller was a registered nurse. Sometimes she stayed home all day, but more often she was gone for a week or even more, living around the clock with an elderly at-home patient.

Mr. Eller was a banker, but he also served on city council—which meant he dashed off to meetings at weird hours.

"Go on up and see," Mrs. Eller called over her shoulder to Stuart, waving her hand in the direction of the stairway.

Stuart loved the Ellers' house. Or, more specifically, he loved the way they did things. Loose. Easy. Practical.

Stuart's own mother wouldn't even let a girl stick her big toe in his room, much less barge in and wake him up. It wasn't allowed. She worried he'd try some of that junk on TV—the R-rated stuff that flashed across the screen at the exact second she walked by.

Nothing Stuart said would convince her that he didn't have enough nerve to hold a girl's hand, much less kiss her face off. Besides, Mack wasn't a girl, at least not *that* way. She was more like a big sister. And friend.

"You're growing up," Stuart's mother argued all the time. "And Mackenzie's older. Besides, having *any* girl in your room is a bad idea. Period. End of discussion."

Yeah, right, thought Stuart. Like there was a parade of girls lining up outside his bedroom door just dying to see his dirty socks and battery-powered dragon.

Stuart knocked softly on Mack's bedroom door.

No answer.

He knocked harder, then leaned closer.

"Mack," he whispered into the doorknob.

"Mack!" shouted a loud voice so close behind him that Stuart got major whiffs of bacon breath.

Stuart jumped, slamming his head, *Blam!* into the door. He whirled around. "Dillinger!" he cried out, rubbing his head where it had already begun to throb.

"Hey, Stuey," oozed Dillinger in the mocking tone he'd spent fourteen years perfecting. "What's up, little guy?"

Dillinger was one of Mack's older brothers. The one Stuart couldn't stand. Mainly because he always called him Stuey. And "little guy."

"Mack!" he shouted again. "Stuuuuuuuuuuuey's here."

Mack's door flew open. She gave her brother a poisonous look and pulled Stuart into the room.

"What the—?" she exclaimed, staring at him. Her face still had sheet creases carved into her cheeks.

"Sorry," mumbled Stuart, suddenly feeling stupid that he'd showed up so early on a Saturday morning.

Mack didn't have on the blue pajama bottoms covered in clouds that he'd seen her wearing three years ago. One, because she'd obviously outgrown them. And two, because they hadn't even been pajama bottoms. They'd been weird pants—just like all the other wacky clothes that Mack wore every single day.

Right now, she had on some kind of long, crimson, kimono-looking thing with Chinese writing all over the back.

Stuart gazed around Mack's room. He loved all her weird stuff. It had to be the most random clutter collection on Earth. Every inch held something strange: a tiny skull on one corner of her desk, a giant spiky red plant on the floor in front of her closet, a medieval tapestry on the wall beside her bed. Crystals, candles, a big cylinder that sounded like a rain forest when you turned it upside down, an ostrich egg, green rubber boots with frog faces, a clear glass vase filled with sand from the Mojave Desert, a bamboo flute, a tiny vial of water from a melted glacier, two dozen plastic ants, and a cowboy hat. The medieval wall hanging was Stuart's favorite because it had two dragons on it.

Mack crawled back into bed and pulled her poofy purple comforter up to her chin. Her chewed-to-the-quick fingernails peeked over the edge. "What's your mother done now?" she asked with a grin.

"How'd you know?"

"ESP." She gazed sympathetically at Stuart.

"I can't do anything without getting busted," he said pitifully.

"Tell me what I *don't* know."

"I'm so sick of it," he grumbled, picking up a stack of magazines piled in one of those girly upholstered bedroom armchairs. He dumped them onto the floor and flopped into the undersized seat. "I'm always grounded, and now she's taken my computer away—except for doing homework."

"So," said Mack, sliding out of bed and standing up. "Fix it."

She stretched toward the ceiling. Her arms weren't skinny anymore. In fact, physically, she was nothing like her ten-year-old self, except for the same supersmooth straight red hair. No. Thirteen-year-old Mackenzie had morphed into what all his friends called *hot*.

Stuart was not clueless about the change—it just didn't affect him. Mack was Mack. Totally there as a friend. Majorly out-of-reach as a babe.

She reached down and tugged her rumpled sheets straight. They were covered with stuff from *Star Wars*—Luke wielding a light saber, Darth Vader's black skull-shaped head, a shaggy-but-smiling Chewbacca, and lots of little R2D2s.

Stuart laughed and loudly tah-dah-dah-*dah*-dummed the theme song.

In one quick jerk, Mack pitched her purple comforter over the sheets. "My brothers' castoffs," she complained.

Stuart stopped singing.

"I like *Star Wars*," he said.

"Me, too." Mack made a face. "But not to sleep on."

"Well," Stuart tried to sound sympathetic, "it could be worse, you know."

"Yeah? Name something."

"Dillinger's old Buzz Lightyear blanket," he reminded her. "The one his hamster died on."

Stuart dropped to the floor and began twitching like a dying rodent.

Mack laughed and threw her pillow at him.

Stuart grinned, then climbed back into the chair and tried to remember what they'd been talking about. Oh, yeah. Mack had said she knew how to fix the problem with his mother.

"So?" he asked. "How am I supposed to get Mom off my back?"

Not that he thought anything would help. Stuart was convinced he'd get caught for everything he did until he was thirty, or until his mother died, whichever came first.

"*You* know," she said, scooping up a bunch of brightly colored pillows and tossing them onto her bed.

"No, I don't."

"Sure you do."

Stuart groaned. "Not that."

"Yep," said Mack. *"That."* Carefully, she centered a large stuffed-animal aardvark in front of the pillows.

"It's a dumb idea," he said to her back.

Mack turned around slowly, placed her hands on her

hips, and looked at Stuart. "How many of my dumb ideas have saved your butt? Huh? How many?"

Stuart stared at the scuffed toes of his soccer shoes. Tons of examples flooded his mind, like the time Mack taught him that club soda would get pizza stains out of his carpet. Or her name association tricks that helped him ace his states-and-capitals test. And then there was the time she convinced his mother that the boy pitching pinecones at cars couldn't possibly have been Stuart, even though he had on his shirt.

"A lot," Stuart mumbled. Gently, he kicked at the plaid tote bag full of rocks that leaned against her dresser.

"You're late," said Mack.

"Huh?" Stuart looked at his sports watch.

Nine-twenty. Soccer practice started at nine-thirty. A fifteen-minute walk.

He turned and bolted. "Gotta go!"

"Think about it!" Mack called after him.

It? thought Stuart. Oh, yeah. *It*—Mack's goofball idea about how to get his mother to chill. The idea that made him want to throw up every time he thought about it.

Well, he couldn't think about it now. He needed to think about getting to practice on time. If he was late, Coach would make him run extra laps. But the only way he'd make it to the soccer field on time was to run.

Either way, he'd have to run. Lose–lose.

He flew down the stairs, jumping three at a time, rounded the corner of the stairway, and slammed into Jordan.

Sploosh. A ripe banana splattered the floor. "Hey! What's the big deal? That was my breakfast."

"Sorry! Gotta go! Late for practice!" Stuart cried, barely slowing down.

"You want a ride?" Jordan yelled after him.

Stuart stopped. He turned and stared at Jordan, Mack's oldest brother. He was tossing his car keys up in the air and catching them.

A ride. The answer to his prayers. Except he wasn't allowed to ride with Jordan. His mother had said so. "No getting in any car, any time, driven by anyone under the age of twenty-one. Period. End of discussion."

Jordan was eighteen.

What could Stuart do?

"Yeah," he blurted. "I'd love a ride."

Stuart slumped down in the duct-taped seat on the passenger side of Jordan's nine-year-old Honda. He kicked aside two empty Gatorade bottles and a Wendy's hamburger bag to make room for his feet. Closing his eyes, he prayed silently, *please don't let Mom see me.* He opened his eyes, glanced nervously up and down Peach Street while Jordan backed out of the driveway. Then he closed his eyes again and added, *or any of her friends.*

Jordan reached over and opened the glove compartment, pulled out a pack of Marlboros and a disposable lighter, and said, "Don't tell my dad. Okay?" Then he lit a cigarette and sucked smoke into his lungs.

Oh, man, thought Stuart, tacking one more request onto his prayer. *Pleeeeze don't let me smell like cigarettes.*

But all he said to Jordan was, "Sure. No problem." Then he rolled down his window.

Jordan shared the Honda with Jefferson, his brother. In all, there were three boys in the Eller family. Dillinger, fourteen. Jefferson, sixteen. And Jordan, the oldest. All of them had red hair like their mother's—rust-colored and kind of kinky. Mack's was red, too, but hers was dark and smooth, like a fancy polished table. And they all had last names for first names.

That's where "call me Mack" had come from. Mackenzie hated it that her parents had tagged them all with what she called excessive names. She claimed it just showed that they never meant to call them or pay any attention to them.

Glancing sideways, he watched the end of the cigarette glow red as Jordan took another drag. He was amazed that Jordan wanted to hide the habit from his dad. After all, wasn't he eighteen? Couldn't he do anything?

Stuart sighed. It was one more discouraging bit of proof that he wouldn't have a life before he was thirty. Maybe fifty.

"Hey, Wyrm," said Jordan, after they'd ridden two blocks. "You any good?"

Jordan called him *Wyrm*, after the dragon in *Beowulf*, the book Jordan was reading for AP English. It actually meant "dragon" in Old English, or Gaelic, or some other thousand-year-old language.

Jordan had explained to him that it was pronounced "worm," in spite of the y. Just like regular English.

Stuart loved it. He'd even changed his e-mail address from "dragonboy" to "wyrm." That had been Mack's idea. She said it made him sound cooler.

And lately, he'd spent hours creating wyrm.com. His own Web site, full of awesome graphics and stuff about beasts. Until his mom had vaporized his computer.

"Earth to Wyrm. You going to answer me?"

"Huh?" said Stuart.

"You any good?" Jordan repeated.

"Good at what?" Stuart answered.

"Soccer."

"Oh. Kind of. Yeah. No. I don't know . . . decent."

"What position you play?"

"Forward."

"Striker? Wing?"

"Wing."

"Score many goals?"

"Sometimes."

"Ha!" said Jordan, pulling over to the curb to let

Stuart out. "I bet you're good." Stuart grinned. How could Jordan and Dillinger be related?

"Thanks for the ride," said Stuart, sliding out of the car.

Mrs. Delgado pulled up behind them to drop off Mike. Mrs. Delgado was Stuart's mother's closest friend.

She waved.

Stuart groaned. He was so busted!

Now, he'd have to start thinking about *it* after all.

3

CLEATS, BUT NO HELMETS

Saturday morning. Nine twenty-eight. Soon to be busted.

Stuart had made it to soccer practice with two minutes to spare.

Had Mrs. Delgado seen him climbing out of Jordan's car?

Of course she had.

Would she tell his mother?

Of course she would.

"Listen up!" Coach J shouted to the pack of seventh-grade boys that was goofing off on the other side of the soccer field.

Stuart and Mike sprinted over to join them.

"We've got a lot to do today," Coach explained. "Anybody want to guess what?"

They all glanced around.

No one answered.

Stuart was still worrying about Mrs. Delgado and what she would tell his mother.

"Okay, guys. Clear out the cobwebs and think back. Two days ago. Our last game."

"But Coach," whined Jeff, adjusting the ratty orange baseball cap that he always wore turned backward. "We won."

"Yep." Coach smiled. "We did. Anybody remember what the score was?"

"Ten-seven!" shouted a bunch of confident voices.

"Louder," said Coach, cupping his ear.

This time Stuart joined in. "Ten to seven!" he yelled proudly. Two of those goals had been his.

"Ten to seven," Coach repeated, then pursed his lips and rubbed his chin with his thumb and forefinger, as if he were trying to figure out something complicated.

He stared at the team's shoes. "Cleats," he said, nodding wisely, as if that were a good thing. Then he glanced up at everyone's heads. "But no helmets," he mused, shaking his head and continuing to rub his chin.

"Aw, come on, Coach." Robert twisted the bottom of his worn-out *I Went to the Super Bowl* T-shirt. Robert's dad took him to awesome places like that all the time. "This is soccer," he groaned, "not football."

Stuart winced. Suddenly, he knew what was coming.

"Exactly!" exclaimed Coach, satisfied. "But ten to seven sure sounds like a football score to me."

Several groans oozed from the pack.

One, "Duh."

"Okay," said Coach, "I'm thinking two-zip sounds like a soccer score. Not ten-seven."

"Or four to two," suggested Jason.

Coach pumped his arm in approval. He wasn't a big guy, but he had muscles. He was lean—in shape.

"So," he said, "What're we going to work on today?"

"Defense!" shouted nineteen Oak Park Warriors.

Coach's laugh pierced the air—a genuine, happy sound. "Okay! Now, let's get on with our warm-ups, then two laps around the field. Then—"

"*Defense!*" everyone finished the sentence for him.

Stuart loved soccer. It even blocked out his worries about getting caught for riding in Jordan's car.

He bent one knee, stretched his other leg behind him, and pushed down. Groin stretch.

Coach J was cool. He always helped his players figure out stuff for themselves.

Stuart counted to ten.

Mike was next to him, trying to touch his toes. Mike's last name, Delgado, meant "thin" in Spanish. Which was a laugh because Mike was huge. Not fat—just big.

"*Thin?*" Coach had teased him once, laughing and shaking his head. "*Delgado* means 'thin'? So what's the Spanish word for 'wide'?"

"*Ancho,*" Mike answered proudly.

So now, whenever he made an awesome defensive play, everybody called him "Ancho Honcho."

Stuart nudged Mike with his knee. Mike, still bent over trying to reach his toes, fell forward.

"Hey!" he complained, jerking up and looking ready

to punch somebody. Then he saw Stuart, grinning stupidly and shrugging as if to say, *who me?* He laughed.

They did side stretches next, with Mike punching his fist close to Stuart's head every time he reached left.

"Paybacks," joked Mike.

Stuart snorted and ducked.

"Today is soccer," said Coach, cutting his eyes at Mike and Stuart, "not boxing."

Stuart smiled knowingly. It wouldn't have surprised him if Coach *had* let them box. He remembered the time Coach had asked everyone to wear sneakers to practice instead of cleats.

"What's up, Coach?" they'd all asked.

Coach J hadn't answered. He'd just herded them all over to the outdoor basketball court.

"Guys," he'd said. "How about we take a day off and shoot some hoops?"

Everybody looked confused, then shrugged. Sure. Why not?

It beat what they'd been expecting—which was about a million don't-bunch-up drills. Coach had spent most of their last game yelling from the sidelines, "Spread out! Play your positions! Move to space!"

So they played basketball, taking turns. Half the guys watched while the other half played. Coach gave them no instruction.

"Just play," he'd said. "Have fun."

And they did. Stuart guarded Jeff, who spotted Mike open under the basket and fired him a low bounce pass that he dropped in for two.

Then Stuart dribbled up court, closely guarded by Jeff, who was in his face, deliberately belching onion fumes from the hot dog he'd eaten for lunch.

"Gross," complained Stuart, waving away the stink. Jeff could be funny, but most of the time he was a jerk.

"Over here!" yelled Robert, breaking free from Mike and waving his arms along the sidelines to the left of the key. Stuart lobbed him the ball, which he tossed up and in for a three-pointer before Mike could get back in position.

The defense got pretty lousy. Everybody was having too much fun running up and down the court, spreading out and finding an open spot so someone would throw them the ball and let them prove what scoring wonders they were.

By the time practice was over, everyone was out of breath, but happy.

"Thanks, Coach!"

"That was awesome."

"Good break."

"Sure," said Coach, dismissing the appreciation with a wave of his hand.

Everyone began grabbing up their jackets, ready to leave.

"Uh," Coach casually scratched his head. "Anybody notice anything?"

The Oak Park Warriors looked at each other.

"Taking a break from soccer drills is good for morale?" Mike suggested.

"Yeah. Anything else?" asked Coach, looking totally satisfied, even though no one had a clue what they'd done right.

They all replayed the afternoon in their heads. Basketball. Shooting. Laughing. Scoring. Goofing off.

"Hanging out helps us be better team players?" asked Stuart.

"Yep." Coach punched the air with his right fist, thumb up. "What else?"

They all fidgeted, stared at their sneakers, and thought some more.

Spreading out. Breaking free for the pass. Calling to each other whenever they were open.

Oh.

All the stuff Coach had been screaming at them to do on the soccer field for a month.

"Oh, man," groaned Mike. "I get it."

"Hey!" exclaimed Jeff, waving his arms. "Soccer's just like basketball."

"You doofus," said Jason, grabbing the grungy base-ball cap that Jeff never took off. Stuart figured he probably slept in it.

"Give me that," Jeff shouted, lunging for his hat.

Jason tossed it to Stuart, who handed it back to Jeff, who brushed it off like it had cooties now, and glared at Jason.

"Well," said Coach. "Some things are similar. Did everybody get it?"

"Yeah," they admitted. "We got it."

"Just don't start dribbling with your hands. Okay? Soccer refs tend to frown on that."

"Yeah, yeah," they'd all muttered as they wandered off to wait for the after-school activities bus, pretending to be bummed out over Coach J's lesson.

But secretly, Stuart walked away excited about the next practice . . . spreading out, getting open, scoring. He could totally *see* it now. He'd bet the rest of the team could, too.

Stuart did one more side stretch and switched his mind back to *this* practice. He bent over, clasped his ankles, and counted to ten. Then he shook out his legs and began to jog around the track with the rest of the team.

"Still grounded?" Robert ran beside him. His dark, spiky hair had that wet look girls thought was cool.

"Yeah," Stuart answered.

"Man," said Jason. "That sucks."

"Yeah," said Stuart, speeding up. He didn't want to talk about all his stupid restrictions.

He sucked in a deep chestful of air, smelling leaves.

The turning-to-bright-colors kind. He thought the orange, red, and yellow ones in the fall had a crisper smell than the summer green ones.

And, it was Stuart's favorite temperature. Not too cold, but definitely nippy. That meant he could run all morning and not have a heat stroke.

Stuart loved running—*if* he could dribble a soccer ball while he was doing it. Flying down the field, guiding the ball with his feet, pushing back the wind with his body. It just didn't get any better than that.

So what if he got caught for riding with Jordan? What more could his mom do? He was already grounded. And computerless. There wasn't anything else he cared about.

After all, she couldn't take away soccer.

Stuart slowed. His heart pumped an extra beat.

Could she?

4

NO SOCCER?

After soccer practice, Stuart charged into his house, banging the front door into the foyer wall, feeling totally pumped about his game. He'd scored three goals during scrimmage, and Coach had only yelled at him once for dribbling the ball all the way downfield without passing it.

Stuart had completely forgotten that Jordan had given him a ride. And that Mrs. Delgado had seen him.

As soon as he saw his mother, he remembered.

Stuart's mom was not in dragon mode, though. It was worse. She was sitting on the sofa in the den, hunched over, with her hands covering her face.

Stuart began to tiptoe, backward, out of sight.

His mother looked up, her eyes red. She'd been crying.

"Stuart," she whispered. "How could you?"

"How could I what?" hedged Stuart, still inching backward in the general direction of the door.

"Ride with Jordan."

I am so busted, thought Stuart.

"Marie Delgado called," his mom continued, sadness filling her voice, "to tell me it was my turn to bring oranges to your soccer game. She said she saw you . . ." Mom stopped talking and sagged like a rag doll. Limp. Worn out. Beaten.

Stuart felt a twinge of guilt.

Then, suddenly, she grew, like a giant balloon in the Macy's parade being pumped full of air.

Stuart felt a twinge of fear.

He watched as she sat up straight, squared her shoulders, and looked him dead in the eye.

Oh, no, thought Stuart. *Dragon Woman.*

"O-o-okay. L-l-look," stammered Stuart, "I forgot—"

"You forgot!" roared his mother.

"No, I mean, I mean . . ."

Stuart had no idea what he meant, but he knew that "I forgot" was the dumbest thing he'd said this week. Maybe this year. Not only was it dumb, it was a lie. He knew it and Dragon Woman knew it. Like he could forget a rule that she'd practically tattooed onto his brain.

"As if you could forget a rule that I practically tattooed onto your brain!" she screeched.

"I'm sorry," said Stuart. "Really, I am. *Real* sorry. I didn't forget. What I meant to say was that I . . . I . . ."

That I *what*? he wondered. That I'm stupid? That I acted without thinking? That it's a dumb rule anyway?

That all my friends are allowed to ride with people who are eighteen? For cripes sake, it's not like Jordan *just* got his license. He's been driving for two whole years.

"You're already grounded," his mother said in a firm voice, but it sounded more like she was talking to herself than to Stuart. "And you're not allowed to e-mail your friends or play video games." She looked up at him, still half angry, but the other half seemed sad. "What else can I take away?" she asked.

"Nothing," he blurted frantically.

"I suppose I could make you quit soccer," she said, gently pulling on her lower lip with her thumb and index finger, as if she were thinking about something she wanted to add to her grocery list.

"No!" Stuart shouted.

"And why not?" she bristled. "Give me one good reason *why not*? I work all day. I try to make a home for the two of us. I try to keep you healthy, safe, out of trouble—"

Her voice got all quivery, as though she might be about to cry again.

"—and *you*. You can't seem to do anything except what I tell you *not* to!"

"Please," begged Stuart. "This morning, I was about to be late for soccer practice, and Jordan offered me a ride. I should have said no. Next time I will say no. Don't make me quit soccer. Okay? Please?"

Stuart held his breath.

"I don't know," answered his mother, shaking her head back and forth vigorously. "I just don't know. . . ."

She stood straight up in the middle of her sentence and marched out of the room.

Stuart stayed there for a full minute, staring blankly at the empty room, clenching and unclenching his fists as they hung by his sides.

Framed pictures crowded the mantel, the bookshelves, the lamp tables. All filled with photographs of him— playing soccer, wearing a fireman's hat when he was three, riding a pony when he was six.

The only picture that wasn't of Stuart was a small one of his dad—a tall, grinning man with dark curly hair, proudly standing beside a sailboat, the sun in his eyes. Except for having the same hair, the man was squinting way too much for Stuart to tell if they looked alike. Someday, Stuart hoped he'd grow that tall, but he doubted it.

His dad had died when he was still a baby, of some routine operation that his mom said the surgeon botched—but she couldn't prove it. Appendix? Gall-bladder? Stuart didn't remember, and his mother wouldn't talk about it. Ever.

Stuart trudged upstairs to his room.

No soccer, he thought, flopping across his bed, knocking the game cartridge that he'd borrowed from Robert to the floor. Flame Blaster. It was awesome. Ten levels of flying on a majestic dragon, shooting fire breathers and defending against creature attacks from a million directions.

He reached down and shoved it under his bed so his mother wouldn't see it.

Stuart wasn't allowed to play violent video games.

How could you have a *non*violent dragon?

Well, there was one, thought Stuart. *The Reluctant Dragon.* Only it wasn't a game. It was a book that his mother had given him when he was six, about a dragon who'd rather write poetry than fight.

It sounded lame, but it was actually a cool story. He'd asked her to read it aloud practically every night. Stuart had loved it—when he was six. But he was twelve now, and it would make a very wimpy video game.

Stuart stretched out across his bed. *No soccer*, he thought again.

Would she really make him quit? What, exactly, was she thinking? No soccer for a week, or no soccer for the rest of the season?

He couldn't quit soccer for a few days and then just show back up. He'd be kicked off the team. What would he tell his friends? What would he tell Coach?

And what was the matter with his stupid mother, anyway? Parents didn't take sports away from their kids. Soccer's a good thing. Like school. It's healthy, educational, character building. Was she nuts?

Stuart shook his head. His mother might be strict, but she did come to his games, and actually got excited when he played well. She also made him Jell-O when he was sick, and Heath Bar shakes when he got better.

Didn't that mean she cared?

"Of course she cares," Mack had told him, but she had a theory. She claimed that Stuart's mom was cursed with an obsessive-compulsive disorder. Like those people who have to wash their hands every two seconds, or empty a wastebasket every time it gets half a Kleenex tissue in it.

Only the wacko thing that Stuart's mom was fixated on was making rules and catching him breaking them. According to Mack, she couldn't help it. It was a disease.

Which is where Mack's other theory came in.

"Except for obsessing over you," Mack had carefully explained, "she doesn't have a life."

As much as Stuart hated to admit it, Mack was probably right. Which meant that he needed a plan to get his mom off his back, and he needed it now.

Mack, of course, had a plan. But it was way too crazy.

What if he just tried being really good? After all, if he didn't break any rules, there'd be nothing to catch him at.

Stuart flipped over onto his back and began listing Mom's rules in his head.

No late-night Comedy Channel.

No riding in cars with anyone under twenty-one.

No smoking.

No sneaking out.

No girls in his room.

Heck. He could live without doing all those things. A couple of them were even reasonable. But what about the others?

No grades below a B.

No R-rated movies

No hanging out at the mall.

No playing Dungeons and Dragons (*that* would turn him into a serial killer).

No violent video games (same reason).

No owning a skateboard.

No telephone calls after 9:00.

No TV on weeknights.

No soda with caffeine.

No breathing.

Okay, he had made the last one up, but she'd think of it sooner or later.

Stuart jerked the pillow off his bed and flung it at the wall. He swept one leg across the books and papers spread over the bottom third of his bed, knocking them all to the floor.

For a second, he wondered why Mom didn't bug him more about his messy room. Ha! he answered himself. Even dragons can't breathe fire *all* the time.

Reaching down, Stuart scooped up the black-and-white carton that landed on the top of the pile. It was the empty box that the replacement ink cartridge for his printer had come in.

Yeah, right! he thought. Who needs ink? I'm not even allowed to turn my computer on. What would I print?

He scanned the writing on the box.

CAUTION:

Do not store in high or freezing temperatures.
Do not touch the green chip
Do not drink.

Do not drink!

Stuart laughed out loud. Who wrote this? My mother?

Stuart crumpled the box in his fist and flung it across the room.

He was ready for Mack's plan.

5

FREE-ME-FROM-MY-IMPOSSIBLE-PARENT

Monday morning at school, Stuart looked everywhere for Mack, but he didn't spot her until noon—lunch break. She was standing in the hall, wearing a purple long-sleeved T-shirt. The sleeves ended in a mass of bell-shaped lacey stuff that drooped over her fingers.

Three ninth-grade jocks were hitting on her.

"Okay, Mack," said Stuart, pulling her between two rows of lockers. The older guys looked like they couldn't decide whether to punch him out or babysit him, but Stuart didn't care. He was desperate.

"I'm ready," declared Stuart.

"Ready for what?" Mack emphatically waved off her fan club, then pulled her straight red hair back into a ponytail and snapped a rubber band around it. Stuart had no clue how she could do that and not tangle her floppy sleeves in it.

"It," he whispered.

"*It?*"

"You know."

"So." Mack grinned. "Finally. You're sure?"

"Yep." Stuart slapped the side of a locker for empha-sis, only he didn't feel quite that forceful on the inside.

Mack's free-me-from-my-impossible-parent idea was a move of sheer desperation. He hated everything about it, but he didn't think he had any choice. Mack was con-vinced that all Stuart's parent problems would go away if his mother had a boyfriend.

There. That was *it*. Her idea. Such as it was—pukey.

But, pukey or not, if a boyfriend for Dragon Woman would give him his life back, Stuart was ready to go for it.

Basically, Mack claimed that Jamie Ellis had too much time on her hands, and what she did with that time was to put Stuart under surveillance that the FBI would envy.

"If she had a *love interest*," Mack argued, "she'd be busy cooking candle-lit dinners and buying lip-gloss that made her look hot. She would *not* be rummaging around under your bed searching for Nuclear Dragon Wars and soda with too much caffeine."

At first, Stuart thought Mack had lost her mind. *Hot?* His mother? No way. Besides, the thought of her with a guy was creepy. He didn't know why, it just was. But now, with soccer at stake, he was willing to try anything.

"This is so great!" said Mack, slapping the same locker that Stuart had. "I know the perfect guy."

"Huh?"

"The guy. You know—for your mother to date."

"What?" Stuart was confused. "Can't she find her own guy?"

"Stuart, she's been single for eleven years. Has she ever dated once?"

"I don't know. A couple of times when I was little. Maybe." Stuart tried hard to remember. "Not lately."

"So, were you planning to ask your fairy godmother to make a boyfriend out of a pumpkin and some rats?"

"No." Stuart rolled his eyes. Sometimes Mack wasn't half as funny as she thought she was.

"My Uncle Joe would be perfect," she announced proudly.

"I don't know your Uncle Joe," Stuart complained.

"That's okay," answered Mack. "Normally, I'd say you should find someone who already likes you. Single guys aren't always crazy about women with kids, you know. But, not to worry. I'll tell him you're cool."

Stuart sighed. "I thought the idea was for him to like *her*, not *me*."

"Oh, he'll love your mom," Mack insisted.

"Yeah, and who told you that?" Stuart grumbled. "*Your* fairy godmother?"

"*Teen People.*"

"What ten people?"

"'Teen,' silly, not 'ten.' It's a magazine. Don't you know anything?"

"No," said Stuart, "I don't." He was hating this more every minute.

"Sorry," said Mack, sympathetically. "I get carried away sometimes. *Teen People* is a magazine, and the last issue had a quiz called 'Making the Perfect Match.' I wrote in answers about your mom and my uncle, and they scored a nineteen! That means they're 'a perfect pair.' They would've needed twenty points to be 'made in heaven.'"

Sometimes Stuart thought Mack talked like an alien. But he actually had a clue this time, because she'd done the magazine thing to him before. Once she made him take a quiz called "Find Your Friendship Style." He had to answer questions like,

> When picking out clothes, do you dress
> a. To impress
> b. For success
> c. For comfort

When he'd answered, "none of the above," she said, "Come on, Stuart, think. Something makes you choose the clothes that you wear."

He'd looked down to see what he had on. A faded green T-shirt and baggy cargo pants.

Not once had Stuart ever thought about why he wore those clothes, but, just to make Mack happy, he thought about it.

"So I won't be naked," he answered.

Mack threw the magazine at him.

Sometimes there was no figuring girls.

The only quiz he had ever liked was "What's Your Cookie Personality?" The questions were all dumb, but the results were amazingly right. He was a chocolate chip cookie: loyal and dependable. Mack was a Thin Mint: cool, sophisticated, and full of energy.

She wasn't overly goofy about girl stuff, though, like some of her mindless friends who hung out in packs and obsessed over the latest CD. Mack listened to hot new boy bands, but she bought Beethoven, too. And, yeah, she took quizzes in teen magazines, but she also read *National Geographic*. Actually *read* it, not just looked at the pictures.

Even Stuart's mom approved of Mack most of the time, probably because Mack liked to hang out and talk to her about the things she sold in her shop—prints, bookends, candles, and stuff.

"You know," Mrs. Ellis had said, "Mack is amazing. It's hard to believe she's only thirteen. She's so . . . so interesting. In an eclectic sort of way."

Stuart had no idea what "eclectic" meant, but Mack was definitely interesting. And amazing. That's why he liked her. That, and the fact that she helped him stay clued-in about things that were years away from being inside his brain-bank.

Things like, what is sushi? Which theater cashiers don't check IDs for R-rated movies? How many feet to the ground does a baby giraffe drop when it's born? What do the punch lines of some dirty jokes mean?

"How come you know so much?" Stuart had asked her once.

"Three older brothers, two hands-off parents, and I read a lot," she'd answered. "It's the same as taking an AP course in Life."

She never acted stuck up about it, though, and mostly, she tried hard not to make him feel stupid. She thought dragons were supercool and she laughed when he burped the "Star-Spangled Banner." How could anybody not like Mack?

On the other hand, Stuart had no clue why Mack liked *him*.

"So," said Mack, interrupting his thoughts, "w hy'd you change your mind?"

"Huh?"

"Your mind," she repeated. "What'd your mother do to change it?"

"She's threatening to make me quit soccer."

"Quit soccer!" Mack's mouth fell open.

"Yeah."

"Soccer's good for you!" She put her hands on her hips. The floppy sleeves covered her fingertips.

"I know." Stuart fell back against a locker, feeling more depressed by the minute. "But she hasn't said, 'Period. End of discussion,' yet."

"Well, that's good," said Mack, but she didn't seem particularly relieved. She raised her left thumb to her mouth and began to gnaw on the nail.

Stuart shook his head. "I doubt it," he said. "I think the only reason she hasn't decided is because it's her turn to bring oranges to this afternoon's game. She feels obligated to the team—not me. As soon as the game's over, I figure I'm out of there."

Mack leaned against the wall. Her eyes blinked four times in a row.

Stuart wondered what was coming—a good thing or a bad thing?

"Okay," she announced. "I'll get Uncle Joe to come to your game today—to meet the orange lady . . . and you."

A bad thing.

"Mack," moaned Stuart, "I'm not sold on this Uncle Joe thing. Can't she find her own boyfriend? Or how about somebody I know . . . and like?"

Stuart pictured his mother holding hands with a strange man. The strange man slipped his arm around her waist and grinned like a cartoon crocodile. The thought made him want to barf.

"Stuart," Mack tilted her head sympathetically. "You need to work through how you feel about this."

Mack was always bugging him to "get in touch with his feelings."

"I feel sick," he said, gripping his stomach.

"No, I mean how you feel about your mom having a boyfriend."

Hadn't he just told her? *He felt sick.* How come he'd never been able to answer that question right?

Maybe he could show her. Stuart stuck his finger down his throat and made gross gagging sounds.

"Oh, please." Mack laughed, rolling her eyes. "Just wait until you meet Uncle Joe. You'll love him!"

She turned and scurried off to lunch before he could answer. "See you at the game," she called over her shoulder.

Stuart groaned. He might like Uncle Joe. But he wasn't going to love him.

6

SHAKE IT OFF

Stuart focused on getting ready to play the Fairfield Cougars. He stretched. He did jumping jacks. He headed the soccer ball, over and over again, until Coach shouted, "Stuart! Give it a rest. You're going to get a concussion."

A bald man sat on the first row of the bleachers next to Mack. She waved wildly at Stuart to come over and meet him. Stuart juggled the ball with his feet, then his thighs. He wasn't going to look at Mack *or* her Uncle Joe if he could help it.

His mother was planning to leave her shop early to watch his game, and to bring oranges, but she hadn't showed up yet.

"Okay, guys," shouted Coach. "Huddle up."

They all surrounded Coach for a last-minute pep talk. "Remember. Team play. Look for the open man. Stuart, don't forget to pass. Mike, you cover number fifteen like a Band-Aid. He's their best scorer. All of you, *defend*.

These guys are good, but you're better." He scanned the team, looking everyone in the eye. "Ready?"

"Ready!" they answered.

Robert high-fived Mike and Stuart. Jason high-fived Jeff and Brad. Mike growled low and mean. Robert spit. Stuart pumped his fist.

"Okay, guys! Go get 'em!" shouted Coach.

Stuart charged out onto the field with his teammates.

"They're gonna be toast!" he shouted.

"Burnt," agreed Robert.

"We'll kill 'em," snarled Mike.

The other team won the coin toss and Stuart took his position, crouched and waiting for the opening kick. He loved the feeling. Pumped. Ready.

His team gained control. Robert quickly passed the ball back to a halfback, who kicked it forward to Stuart, who dribbled down the left side. A defender instantly closed in on him. Stuart faked as if he were going to pass the ball forward, but lifted his foot over the ball instead, and flicked it back through his legs. His opponent was left standing as Stuart took off downfield.

"Go, Stuart!" yelled the crowd.

"Pass the ball!" shouted Coach J from the sidelines.

Stuart wanted to see if he could take it all the way, but he spotted Brad open in the middle and passed it off. Brad trapped it, swiveled, then dribbled toward the goal, but two defenders swooped in on him and stole it.

As the ball headed toward the other end of the field, Stuart glanced at the sidelines and saw his mother sitting down between Mack and bald Uncle Joe.

He froze as he watched Mack introduce Joe to his mother, who smiled charmingly at Joe, who smiled charmingly back.

"Let's go!" yelled Robert.

The Warriors had the ball again, and Robert was dribbling up the field. Stuart sprinted out ahead of him, and yelled, "Robert! Over here!"

Robert fired off a high kick that Stuart stopped with his chest. But before he could take control, the ref blew the whistle. "Off sides!"

Stuart slumped. He hadn't been watching his position.

In the next five minutes of play, Stuart lost the ball three times. Each time he glanced at Uncle Joe, who seemed to be consoling his mother for having such a rotten soccer player for a son, by patting her arm.

On the next play, the ref whistled Stuart for holding. The other team was awarded a free kick, and they scored.

Cougars one. Warriors zero.

Coach pulled him out.

"What's the matter with you?" he asked Stuart as he came off the field. "You look like you've never played before."

Stuart shrugged and slumped onto the bench. Shake it off, he told himself.

But when he went back in four minutes later, he couldn't seem to stop himself from glancing at bald, old-looking Uncle Joe grinning at his mother. So Coach took him out for the rest of the half.

At halftime, the score was tied, one-one. Robert had scored with an awesome header.

Uncle Joe carried his mother's cooler of orange slices over to the players' bench. She strolled beside him, smiling politely.

"What's wrong?" she asked Stuart the second she got close. She walked up and placed her hand on his forehead to see if he had a fever.

"Nothing," he mumbled, brushing her hand away as if it were a gnat.

"Hey there, young man!" exclaimed Uncle Joe in an absurdly peppy voice. He stuck out his hand. "I'm Joe Eller. Mackenzie's uncle."

Stuart shook his hand and muttered, "Hi."

Then, the same hand that had patted his mother's arm, reached over and tousled Stuart's curly hair. "Good try, little guy," boomed Uncle Joe too enthusiastically. "I'll bet you eat their lunch in the second half."

Stuart wanted to throw up. Instead he mumbled, "Thanks," and moved as far away from Uncle Joe, his mother, and the oranges as he could get.

"Who's the dude with your mother?" asked Robert, wandering over to Stuart, sucking on an orange slice.

"Mack's uncle," he answered, while "little guy" echoed back and forth between his ears.

"They dating or something?"

"No."

"You sure?"

"Yeah."

"You don't sound sure."

"Geez!" shouted Stuart. "Back off!"

Robert dropped the orange slice. "Man," he said. "What's with you, anyway?"

Stuart sagged. "Sorry."

"What gives?" Robert persisted, picking up the drippy orange wedge and wiping grass off of it.

"Just some dumb idea of Mack's," Stuart answered, trying to sound as if he didn't care.

"Oh." Robert had been friends with Stuart long enough to know about Mack's ideas. "So . . . what's her latest plan?"

"Nothing." Stuart pulled a soccer ball over with his foot and started trapping it, then scooping it up with the top of his foot, over and over.

"Whatever," said Robert, taking a bite of orange and spitting out a piece of grass with it. "You know, you pretty much stunk in the first half."

Stuart ignored him, focusing on his footwork, which moved harder and faster, while Robert waited for him to say something.

"Man," Robert finally blurted, "if Mack's ideas mess

with your head this bad, maybe it's time you got your own ideas."

"Huh?" said Stuart.

"Look. Mack's cool and all. But dude, she runs your life."

Stuart froze. The soccer ball he'd been scooping up bounced and rolled away.

"No, she doesn't."

Robert looked hard at Stuart. "Whatever. You going to get it together in the second half?"

"Yeah," said Stuart, glaring stubbornly back at him, "I am."

"Cool." Robert ambled back over to the orange cooler and grabbed another slice.

Stuart stalked after the ball, grabbed it up, and stomped back to the bench. He slumped by himself on one end, bouncing the soccer ball with both hands, hard, into the ground in front of him.

Uncle Joe and his mother rejoined Mack and the other fans in the bleachers on the other side of the field.

Stuart's brain was whipping thoughts back and forth, like a speed-passing soccer drill. Mack does *not* run my life! Does she? I have ideas! Don't I? Yes! He slammed the ball harder into the dirt between his feet. I *do*. I'm creating my own Web site. Wait, wasn't that Mack's idea? Maybe. But I did it. My site: wrym.com. Whoa. Wasn't naming it that her idea, too. So? I play soccer.

She has *nothing* to do with soccer. Stuart's whole body suddenly drooped. Will I even *be* playing soccer after today?

Stuart stopped bouncing the ball.

I may not even be playing in the second half, he thought.

He stood and booted the ball halfway across the field.

"Okay, guys," yelled Coach. "Listen up. We're going to win! Just keep doing what you're doing. Jason," he turned toward the goalie, "play a few more feet out from the goal—narrow the angle. Just don't do it too soon."

Jason nodded.

"Mike," said Coach, "great job on number fifteen. Robert, keep scoring. Everybody—good teamwork. I'm really proud of you guys. See if you can pass the ball quicker, though. Remember, you don't always have to trap it first."

"Now," said Coach. "Jason, Brad, Jeff, Robert. Get out there. And, Jeff—lose the hat."

Jeff actually jerked his orange cap off eagerly and pitched it under the bench.

Coach reeled off the rest of the names of the starters for the second half.

Stuart wasn't one of them.

He plopped down on the bench and glared across the field at Mack, Uncle Joe, and his mother.

Uncle Joe and his mother. Yuck. The guy was so fakey. And old. What had Mack been thinking?

Stuart wondered for a second if he would hate any guy who hung around his mom. Maybe, but he didn't think so. If it meant getting his privileges back, Stuart thought he could learn to deal—with a cool guy. Uncle Joe was an over-age dork.

Little guy. Who calls a seventh grade jock, *little guy?*

Dillinger. Mack's jerk brother. That's who. Uncle Joe and Dillinger even looked alike. Same smirky grin. Did that mean jerkhood was genetic?

Thweet. The whistle signaled the start of the second half.

"Hey, big guy." Coach plopped down beside Stuart. "You ready to play?"

Stuart jumped up. "Yes!"

"Whoa," said Coach. "Sit down."

Stuart sat.

"You're sure you're ready?"

"Positive!"

Coach looked at him. "What about—?" he stopped. "Never mind. If you say you're ready, you're ready. Next throw-in, you're in." Coach nudged him with his elbow, then got up and stood on the sidelines. "Spread out!" he shouted at the playing field.

Stuart replaced Jeff two minutes later, fired up, fists clenched, focused. "Don't look at the bleachers," he whispered fiercely under his breath. "Just play."

And he did. He dribbled like a pro. He remembered to

pass. He got open. He stole the ball. He took four shots at goal. One was blocked, two went wide, and one soared over the net. The score was still one to one.

"One minute," signaled the ref. The game was almost over.

"Heads up!" shouted Coach from the sidelines. "You can do it!"

Robert kicked the ball to Stuart, who took off downfield. A Cougar defender charged him head on, stripped the ball right out from under his feet, and passed it to a halfback. Stuart ran full speed, caught up with the ball, and executed a slide tackle to boot it back toward Robert. His timing was off.

Thweet! "Tripping!" called the referee. "Free kick, green."

Stuart sagged, then recovered. Shake it off, he told himself. Keep playing. Defend.

Stuart and three teammates formed a defensive wall, shoulder to shoulder, protecting the goal. Jason braced himself for the free kick, which arced high, right, and on target. Jason jumped high and left, catching the ball inches before it penetrated the goal.

Stuart heard the roar of approval from the Warrior fans in the bleachers. He raced back downfield to get in position as Jason booted the ball back into play. Brad headed it to Robert, who passed it to Stuart. He dribbled ten yards, and passed it back. Quick. Crisp. Before a defender could touch him. Then he dropped back, and moved left. "Robert!" he shouted, finding himself open. "Here!"

Stuart watched the pass coming, high. He spotted an opening between himself and the goal, right before the ball bounced in front of him. As it started to rise, he booted a half-volley shot, connecting solidly with his instep. The ball shot low toward the left goal post, bounced once as the goalie dove for it, and landed in the back of the net.

Goal!

Whistle.

End of game.

Incredible! Stuart felt as if he could fly—really fly—straight up into the clouds. Instead, his whole team pretty much slapped, high-fived, and pounded him into the dirt. He loved it.

He jogged off the field. Coach hugged him. Mack and his mother clapped and jumped up and down on the other side of the field. Uncle Joe grinned.

Uncle Joe.

For over thirty minutes, Stuart had blocked out Mack's idea to get his mom a date. He'd even forgotten that this might be his last game. Now, suddenly, it all came back.

The sinking feeling in his gut met the soaring feeling in his chest. Stuart grinned. The soaring feeling won out.

As Stuart made his way toward the car to meet his mother, bunches of friends and fans congratulated him.

When he finally broke free of the crowd, Robert trotted up and fell into step beside him. "Great game, Wyrm."

"Thanks," said Stuart. He loved it when his friends called him Wyrm. "You, too."

"You going to tell me what was bugging you back there?"

"Oh," said Stuart, still grinning over the win, "Mack thinks Mom and her Uncle Joe are the perfect pair," said Stuart.

"Man," said Robert. "How old is that geezer?" Before Stuart could answer, he said, "Your mom should date Coach."

"Coach?"

"Yeah."

"Coach isn't married?"

"Nope," said Robert, veering toward his dad's black Chevy Blazer in the front of the parking lot. "See ya!" he called, opening the passenger door and hopping in.

Stuart stood and watched Robert drive away with his dad. Then he saw his mom's green Subaru wagon. Mack and her uncle were leaning against it, laughing about something with his mother. The weird pinched look his mom seemed to have had on her face ever since he'd turned twelve seemed softer somehow. Maybe she did need a boyfriend.

Just don't make it Uncle Joe, thought Stuart. Then he grinned as he replayed Robert's big newsflash. *Coach isn't married.*

He walked confidently toward Uncle Joe and Mack. She was wearing an orange blouse that looked as though it were made out of that scratchy sack stuff that potatoes come in. She had fastened different-sized safety pins all over it.

As Stuart approached, Mack winked at him, clearly pleased with how her plan was going.

Stuart winked back. He had an idea of his own.

7

PERIOD.
END OF DISCUSSION

Stuart propped his muddy soccer shoes up against the dashboard on the passenger side of his Mom's Subaru, crossed his arms, and waited for her to tell him, one more time, what a great game he'd just played.

He had the ride home with his mom totally figured out. Any minute now, as soon as she finished backing the car out of their parking space, she'd say, "Stuart, you played a fantastic second half. I'm so proud of you."

He'd say, "Thanks, Mom."

Then, when she reached over to squeeze his knee with mom-like pride, he'd say, "We couldn't have won without Robert, though."

"Or you!" she'd brag.

Then Stuart would modestly insist, "It was a team effort."

"You know," she'd say, easing her car into the traffic

on Dogwood Drive, "you're right. It was. But, clearly they need you to be a part of it."

Bingo! Then he'd have her!

All he'd need to say after that was, "Thanks, Mom, I knew you'd never make me quit soccer and let my team down." Stuart's mother was borderline neurotic about not letting people down.

With the unthinkable quit-soccer threat out of the way, he could move on to his new idea—the one that was way better than Mack's.

Heck, forget setting his mom up with Uncle Joe. No. Somehow, Stuart wanted to figure out a way to get her to date Coach.

He hadn't even known that Coach J was single until Robert had told him at the game. He grinned smugly to himself, pushed his dirty cleats firmly against the dashboard, and slid lower in his seat. It was so perfect.

"Take your feet off the dash," said his mother, as she backed their car out of the parking space.

Stuart dropped his feet to the floorboard and sat up straighter.

"Sorry," he said, trying to wipe the mud-caked streaks away with his hand. "How'd you like the game?"

"Loved it," she said. "You were great."

Before Stuart could open his mouth, she added, "Mack wants us to join her family for dinner tonight. They're ordering pizza."

"Huh?" said Stuart.

"Dinner. Tonight. At the Ellers. How about it?"

"No!" he blurted.

She turned to stare at him. "Why? You and Mack are great friends. Both her parents will be there for a change—"

"And Uncle Joe?"

"Who? Joe? Oh, I don't know," said Stuart's mom. "I guess he might be."

"Mom," moaned Stuart. "He's a dinosaur."

"Stuart!" she exclaimed. "What *are* you talking about?"

Stuart jammed his feet back up on the dash. "I don't like him."

"Put your feet down!" shouted his mother. "You don't even know him."

"I know I don't want you to date him."

"Date him!" Stuart's mother stopped the car in the middle of the parking lot. She twisted as far around as her seatbelt would allow, and gaped at Stuart. "Who said I wanted to *date him?*"

"Mom," said Stuart. "You're blocking traffic."

"I don't want to date *anybody!*"

She inched the car forward. "We're going to the Ellers' for dinner," she said firmly. She eased her car out into the traffic on Dogwood Drive, "and I've decided you'll have to quit soccer until you can learn to listen to me. Period. End of discussion."

+++

Stuart sprawled across his bed on his stomach and tried to figure out where he'd messed up. Was it when he'd put his feet on the dash? Or when he'd called Uncle Joe a dinosaur? Did it matter?

Dragon Woman was going to make him quit soccer.

Add to that: grounded for eternity, no computer, no life. *And* a pizza party with Uncle Joe putting old-guy moves on his mother.

Man, thought Stuart, rolling his eyes upward, I've got to be the most in-trouble kid, ever.

He wondered if he could make the *Guinness Book of World Records*. He'd be willing to bet money that no one else had come close to getting busted as many times as he had.

He flipped over on his back, hugging his pillow.

Why me?

All the bad things that Stuart's friends had ever done raced through his mind. How come *they* never got caught?

Last summer, Robert swiped his sister's bike and crashed it off a homemade ramp. Did his parents find out? No. He convinced them that some out-of-control kid taking Driver's Ed had run over it.

Mike blew up his next-door neighbor's mailbox with a cherry bomb. Jeff snuck out in the middle of the night and drove his parents' BMW!

Those were bad things, for Pete's sake!

And what had he done?

Stuart Ellis, juvenile delinquent and grounded for life, had ridden in a car with a licensed driver and watched the Comedy Channel.

It made him want to spit. Except he knew he'd get caught.

Getting busted is what he did best.

He thought back to the car ride with Jordan, who had smoked a cigarette. "Don't tell my dad," he'd said.

Stuart tried to imagine getting away with smoking in his car—if he had a car. Or if he smoked.

His mother would inspect it six times a day, sniffing for telltale signs of cigarettes, beer, and who knows what else. Caffeine, maybe? Girls? Lies? It wouldn't surprise him one bit if she could smell every one of those things.

Too bad she couldn't smell normal, ordinary boy.

She's going to ruin my life forever, he thought.

Stuart balled up his fists and punched his pillow. "No way!"

Three feathers flew up into the air.

Oh yeah? he shot back, swatting the feathers and arguing with himself. What are you going to do to stop her? Mack's birdbrain idea?

Forget that! I've got my own ideas!

Ha! Your mother, Jamie Ellis, doesn't want to date anybody!

Yeah, well, who cares? Coach J wouldn't like her any-way.

No kidding. He's way too cool . . . and nice . . . and . . . and . . . totally unstressed.

Stuart's mother knocked softly on his door, then pushed it open and stepped into the room. "Stuart, honey, it's time to go to the Ellers." She sniffed the air in his room. "And put your dirty soccer clothes in the washing machine," she added, wrinkling her nose.

Stuart glanced around his room for anyone who could possibly be *honey*.

Before he left for the Ellers, Stuart dropped his dirty socks, soccer shorts, and jersey into the washer. His mother had already filled it with water and added the soap powder. When he pulled the dial to start the machine, the agitator thrashed into action. Stuart stared at the churning clothes. They looked exactly like he felt.

Facing pizza night with Uncle Joe made him all jumpy and jittery. Would he have a chance to tell Mack that he hated it? Would she get mad?

How long would he have to watch Uncle Joe try to be charming before he could go home? In time to talk his mother out of making him quit soccer?

What if Dillinger and his uncle both started calling him *little guy*? Would he totally lose it?

Walking to the Ellers' house for dinner, Stuart crossed

Peach Street with his mom and spotted a crow pecking away at a blob of roadkill—probably a squirrel—in the middle of the street.

Stuart figured it was an omen.

His mother strolled ahead of him, wearing jeans and a turtleneck that made her look good for a mom. Usually it made Stuart proud to know that, in spite of her dragon ways, his mom was pretty. But tonight, with Uncle Joe lurking like a horny-toad, he would have preferred her to look like a troll.

"Stuart, honey. Come on," called his mother, motioning him to catch up with her.

Dinner at the Ellers was like life at the Ellers. Laid-back and loud. With a thousand conversations going on at once.

It might have been fun, too, if Uncle Joe hadn't spent so much time chatting up his mother. Or if the night hadn't ended with Stuart being a jerk.

Everyone converged on the family room. His mom sat on the sofa between Uncle Joe and Mrs. Eller, who looked supercomfortable in her gray sweats and running shoes. Mr. Eller still had on his tie from some meeting, but he immediately loosened it and relaxed back in a huge leather recliner. Dillinger and Jefferson spilled out of two armchairs, while Stuart, Mack, and Jordan sprawled on the floor.

Unlike Stuart's living room, there were almost no

pictures. A five-by-seven of a young Mr. and Mrs. Eller, posing at the Grand Canyon, leaned between two stacks of books. Baby pictures of Jordan and Jefferson hung side by side in a corner of the room that housed three hockey sticks, a basketball, and two grocery bags stuffed full of coat hangers.

Five pizza boxes lay open on the coffee table.

Mack leaned in, searching through the boxes. She still had on the funky shirt with the safety pins—a Mack original.

Even if he had the interest, Stuart would never have the nerve to do something like that to his clothes. Besides, what came across as cool and arty on Mack looked stupid on other people.

"Where's the Veggie Special?" she asked, continuing to hunt.

"Uh-oh," said Mrs. Eller, slapping her hands to her checks. "I forgot."

"You forgot?" Mack repeated blankly.

Meanwhile, Mack's three brothers grabbed paper plates and began piling pizza slices onto them as if they hadn't seen food since last Tuesday.

"Get over it," grumbled Dillinger, muscling Mack out of his way.

"Do you want me to order another one?" Uncle Joe asked Mack, sympathetically wrinkling his forehead.

Stuart, annoyed, couldn't help but notice that a

scrunched-up brow, if the whole head is bald, made a lot of creases.

"No," answered Mack, looking appreciatively at Uncle Joe. "Thanks, though."

"Boys!" Mrs. Eller scolded. "Guests first."

"Dillinger!" complained Jefferson. "You took all the pepperoni!"

Uncle Joe, smiling, reached his hand toward Stuart's mother's plate and said, "Jamie, what can I get you?"

Mack, so certain her plan was working, winked at Stuart.

"Did anybody read my letter to the editor?" asked Mr. Eller, reaching for a slice covered with sausage, mushrooms, and onions.

"Thanks," Stuart's mom answered Uncle Joe. "But I'll get it."

Stuart ignored Mack's wink. He was way past ready to tell her *his* idea.

"I did," Mack answered her dad, as she sat back down and waited for the feeding frenzy to finish.

Jefferson snatched a wedge of pizza off Dillinger's plate.

"What letter?" asked Jordan.

"Hey!" yelled Dillinger, showcasing a mouthful of cheese and pepperoni. He threw an elbow that knocked Jefferson sideways into the TV.

"The one about finding a better location for the city's

new landfill," Mr. Eller answered, sipping his iced tea.

"Are you all right?" gasped Stuart's mom, staring at Jefferson.

"Who won the Raiders game?" asked Jordan.

Jefferson regained his balance, wiped spilled tomato sauce off his jeans with his thumb, then licked it. "I'm fine," he said.

"Nobody read it?" boomed Mr. Eller in disbelief.

"The Packers killed them," said Dillinger.

"I read it," Mack repeated.

"Who'd like more tea?" asked Mrs. Eller, getting up.

"Mack read it," said Uncle Joe, nudging Mr. Eller's arm as he followed Mrs. Eller into the kitchen.

"I'm picking them to go all the way to the Super Bowl," said Mr. Eller.

Stuart felt as if he were online, in a chat room. Everyone was talking out of sync, answering something that had been said one or two questions earlier.

Suddenly, Mr. Eller tightened his tie, pulled on his jacket, and left—apologizing for needing to be at a meeting. Jefferson and Dillinger split five minutes later, heading for the mall to check out new CDs.

While Mrs. Eller and Stuart's mom relaxed on the sofa listening to Uncle Joe brag about being a prehistoric football star, Jordan ambled into the kitchen and booted up the computer.

Stuart sat cross-legged on the floor, gnawing miserably

on a chunk of pizza crust and watching Uncle Joe pat his mother's arm for the millionth time.

All he wanted to do was go home.

"What's wrong?" asked Mack, carefully picking sausage off a pizza slice.

"Nothing."

"Right," said Mack sarcastically. "You look like your dog died."

"I don't have a dog."

Mack slid her plate on top of one of the empty pizza boxes, grabbed Stuart's arm, and pulled him, reluctantly, to his feet. She dragged him into the front hall.

"Okay. Give."

"How old's your uncle?" Stuart asked, trying to sound casual, but his insides were starting to jerk like a washing machine again.

"What? Uncle Joe? I don't know. Forty maybe."

"Or ninety," jeered Stuart.

"Huh?" said Mack, stunned.

"Mom's going to date Coach," Stuart announced.

"What?" Mack stared at Stuart. "Doesn't she like Uncle Joe? They seem to be getting along—"

"*I* don't like him," said Stuart firmly. "I like Coach."

"Coach J?"

"Yeah."

"Bad idea," said Mack, shaking her head.

Stuart's face flushed hot. He replayed Robert's remark,

the one about Mack running his life, in his head. "You aren't the only one who has good ideas," he shot back.

"Stuart," said Mack, gazing at him with the same knowing look that his mother always had when *she* ran his life. "You'll regret it if Coach dates your mom. There are too many things—"

"You think you know everything!" he yelled.

"I do not!" said Mack, raising her voice, and flinging up her arms in frustration. "I just think—"

The agitator in Stuart's stomach suddenly stopped, then lurched into the spin cycle. "Well, don't!" he shouted. "Don't think! Not for me." He pointed his finger at her face. "You got that?"

He turned and stormed out the front door.

Just before he slammed it, he wheeled around and yelled, "And those safety pins on your shirt look stupid!"

Halfway home, he felt like an idiot.

8

HOBBIT TOAST

Tuesday morning, Stuart woke up early and immediately pictured Mack's face—the way it had looked right before he'd slammed the door. She'd been blinking fast, but not focused the way she blinked when she was thinking. No. She'd been blinking fast to hold back tears.

Stuart couldn't believe what a jerk he'd been. But he was proud that he'd stood up for himself. What if Robert was right? What if Mack did run his life? Wasn't it time for him to have some ideas of his own?

But he hadn't meant to make her cry. He didn't even know Mackenzie Eller *could* cry. He'd never seen her any way but in control.

"Stuart," whispered his mother, tapping on his bedroom door, "are you awake?"

"No," he answered, pulling the covers up over his head and sliding down between the sheets.

Mom opened the door and entered, holding out a book. "Jordan gave me this last night. He meant to give it to you before you left, but . . ." She hesitated and scrunched her eyebrows together. "When *did* you leave? I hope you thanked Mrs. Eller for dinner."

"Yeah," he lied, reaching for the book. It was a worn hardback copy of *The Hobbit*. "What's this for?"

"Jordan thought you might want to borrow it. He said that it's about the 'most awesome wyrm, ever.'"

Stuart thumbed the pages. Toward the back, he spotted a picture of a sleek red dragon curled on top of a gigantic treasure hoard of sparkling gold and jewels. Smoke curled from both the serpent's nostrils while a small person bowed in front of him. The caption said, "Conversation with Smaug." Skulls of several people, who had apparently not had successful chats with Smaug, littered the floor.

"Smaug," said Stuart, under his breath, wishing he could skip school and start reading. "Cool."

He'd heard of Smaug. He was the ferocious, greedy dragon that terrorized dwarves and men in the prequel to *Lord of the Rings*. The undersized person bravely talking to him in the picture—brave because he was clearly in danger of being toasted like a marshmallow—was a hobbit.

Stuart looked up and remarked to his mother, "Jordan probably figured I needed something to read since I'm not allowed to do anything else." He lowered the book dejectedly, and added, "ever."

"Don't start," warned his mother.

Stuart figured he was about to be toast, just like the hobbit in the picture.

"Mom," he complained anyway, "I have no life."

She sighed. "Of course you have a life."

"Hah!" said Stuart. "I can't work on my Web site, I can't see my friends, not even at soccer. Shoot, I can't even e-mail them."

"You can see them at school," she argued, "and you can talk to them on the phone—before nine o'clock."

"Big deal." Stuart threw up his hands. "Guys don't talk on the phone except to make plans. And I can't make plans because I'm grounded!"

The phone rang across the hall in his mother's room. She wagged a finger at him, said, "Don't raise your voice!" and hurried to answer it.

"Joe!" he heard her say through his open door. "What a surprise!"

Joe? thought Stuart. Uncle Joe? Calling this early?

He hopped out of bed and slipped quickly across the hall, standing hidden just outside his mother's bedroom.

"No, not at all," he overheard. "I've been up. Well, yes. Thank you. I had fun, too."

Was Uncle Joe asking her out? Stuart felt nauseous.

His mom murmured, "umm-hmm," a couple of times. Otherwise, not a word. Uncle Joe must be telling her what a hero he'd been in the Civil War.

"This Saturday?" she said.

Oh no, thought Stuart.

"I don't think so, but I've heard it's a wonderful show. I bet Mack would love to go. It would be a shame to waste the ticket."

She was turning him down! Yes! Stuart flew back to his own room and jumped under the covers.

When his mom returned, she explained, "That was Joe Eller."

Who in the heck calls before breakfast asking for a date? Someone old and desperate, thought Stuart.

"The dinosaur," he muttered.

"What on earth is wrong with you?" exclaimed his mother, frowning. But then she laughed, and said, "I thought you liked dinosaurs."

"Dragons, Mom."

"Ah yes, that's right," she answered. Then she got all stern looking again and said, "Stuart, Joe Eller is a nice man."

"Then how come you're not going out with him on Saturday?" As soon as he'd said it, he wanted to take it back. But it was too late.

"You listened!" shrieked his mom. He had heard her shout plenty of times, but shrieking was new. Her face flushed. Omigosh, he thought, his mother, Dragon Woman, was getting all embarrassed and girly about having a guy call her up.

Gross.

"Mom," said Stuart, changing the subject. "Please don't make me quit soccer."

"Oh, honey," she said, plopping down on his bed and looking wilted. "Do you think I *like* punishing you?"

"Well," Stuart hesitated while he decided the best way to phrase his answer. "Yeah."

"Silly." She squeezed his knee through the covers. "You don't mean that."

Yes, as a matter of fact, he did.

Then she launched into her I'm-only-doing-this-for-your-own-good lecture, followed by an equally amazing this-hurts-me-more-than-it-hurts-you lie. Stuart had both speeches memorized.

As she droned on and on, Stuart wondered if her sermons would last so long that he'd miss school. He glanced at the clock. No such luck. It was still early. Even worse, he felt his chances of talking her out of the soccer ban growing slimmer and slimmer. How was he going to tell the guys on his team? What would he say to Coach?

Reluctantly, he admitted to himself, Mack would know what to do. Too bad she'd probably never speak to him again.

Suddenly, he wanted to kick himself. She wouldn't be around to help him figure out how to get his mom and Coach together, either—clearly something she would be better at than Stuart.

If only he'd paid more attention when Mack had rented the movie *Sleepless in Seattle* and made him watch it
with her. At the time, he'd thought it was just a dumb
chick flick, but the plot did center on this kid who was
trying to hook his father up with Meg Ryan, so she could
become his mother.

How had the boy done it? Stuart couldn't remember,
except that it had something to do with getting them both
to New York City, and to the top of the Empire State
Building, at the same time.

All of which seemed way too complicated for Stuart.

What if he went to the drugstore and flipped through
a bunch of goofy girl magazines until he found one
with an article on "Finding Mom a Mate"? Or maybe,
"Introducing Old People"?

Then it hit him! The perfect solution.

Yes!

Forget talking his mother out of taking soccer away.

Forget having to explain it to Coach.

No.

He would get his mother to go to Coach and tell him
herself. It might not be as killer as the Empire State
Building, but still . . . it could definitely work. Right there
in Coach's smelly gym office, they would fall madly
in love, then Mom would have better things to do than
catch Stuart breaking rules, and he would live happily
ever after.

He was so proud of himself that a smile lit up his face. It was all he could do not to cheer.

"I knew you'd understand," said his mother, smiling gratefully back.

Huh? thought Stuart. Understand what? Oh, yeah. Mom was still listing all her reasons why punishing him was a good thing.

Stuart almost laughed out loud. It didn't matter what she said. His idea was about to fix everything. Yes! And the best part was that he could pull this off without Mack!

Whoa, he cautioned himself, get a grip. Pull yourself together. Sound mature.

"Mom," he said. "I'm really sorry I keep messing up. It won't happen again. I promise."

His mother hugged him.

"And I can use this time to work harder on my school-work."

She gently pushed him back at arm's length and eyed him with suspicion.

Dummy, thought Stuart. Don't overdo it.

"And, this afternoon," he said, holding his breath, "Coach is always in his office right after school. You can explain everything to him then."

Mom laughed and dropped her arms. "Such a kidder." She gave him a playful nudge.

"No, Mom, I mean it. You *have* to go. He'll think I'm

making it up, to get out of practice or something. At school, we always have to have a note from our parents. For everything. You know that."

"Okay, I'll write a note."

"No! He'll think I forged it."

"What *is* the matter with you?" asked Stuart's mom, looking at him as though he'd lost his mind.

"Look," she said, not waiting for him to answer, "I'll write the note. The school doesn't need an explanation, but if you want Coach to have one, you can give it to him yourself."

Then she launched into a take-responsibility-for-your-actions lecture.

Hobbits, thought Stuart, sliding even deeper under his bed covers, aren't the only ones who have conversations with dragons.

He stared hopelessly at the ceiling while his mother underlined her sermon with energetic hand movements.

What, he wondered, would Mack do now?

9

LOWER THAN DIRT

At school, Stuart scanned the halls for Mack. Finally, right before lunch, he saw her, walking between two of her friends, Chelsea and Amy. Mack had on bell-bottom jeans with holes in them, a T-shirt, and a long red scarf dangling around her neck. Two eighth-grade guys leaned against a locker and eyeballed her like she was a hot fudge sundae.

Why had he told her she dressed stupid? She looked great.

"Hey, Mack!" Stuart called. "Wait up."

She kept walking, but it wasn't her usual arm-swinging confident stride. No. She seemed to hesitate, then she quickly turned the corner and vanished.

Amy looked back at him as if he were a giant wad of Red Man chewing tobacco that someone had hocked on the floor.

Fine, thought Stuart. Who needs her?

I do, he answered himself. What the heck am I going to tell Coach?

Stuart had lain awake half the night trying to figure out how to fix his messed-up life. For the first time, he totally understood why the Seattle movie had been called *Sleepless*.

He even wished on a star. And he didn't ask for much either—just his old life back. The one where his biggest worry was remembering to pass the soccer ball.

His mother wouldn't even tell him whether she was making him give up soccer for a week or forever.

"We'll see," she'd said.

"But, Mom—"

"No buts."

Didn't she understand *anything*? How was he supposed to tell Coach, "we'll see"? Coach would have no choice but to scratch him from the roster. Permanently.

After school, Stuart dragged himself to Coach's office. In spite of all the thinking he'd done the night before, he still didn't have a plan. Getting busted was wearing out his brain. He'd have to wing it.

The door stood open, so Stuart stuck his head in. It smelled like file cabinets and old sneakers.

"Stuart," said Coach, glancing up from a stack of papers on his desk. "Pull up a chair."

Stuart slid his book bag off his shoulder, let it drop noisily to the floor, and sat down across from Coach.

"Man," Coach observed. "You look like your dog died."

"I don't have a dog," mumbled Stuart.

"Right. Okay, well . . ." Coach twisted his head quizzi-cally, waiting.

"I'm quitting the team," Stuart said softly, his head drooping halfway to his lap.

"What?" Coach placed his pen down and leaned for-ward, his elbows pressed into the top of his desk.

"I have a note," he said meekly, sliding the piece of paper his mother had given him toward Coach.

Coach snatched it up, scanned it, and asked, "Why?"

"I just have to," Stuart whispered.

"Are you sick?" Coach sounded concerned.

"No."

"Bad grades?"

"No."

"Would you rather not say?"

"No."

"You mean you *do* want to say?"

"Yeah."

Coach waited.

"It's a punishment."

"A punishment?" Coach sounded surprised.

"Yeah."

"Do you want to tell me what you did?"

"No . . . yeah . . . I don't know."

"Stuart," said Coach. "It doesn't really matter. This is between you and your mom. If I can help I will, but—"

"Talk to her," Stuart blurted. "Go talk to her. Please. I

didn't do anything bad, honest. All I did was ride in a car with Jordan Eller, only I'm not supposed to, and a bunch of other stuff that everyone on the planet is allowed to do but me, and—"

"Stuart, I can't tell your mother how to raise her own kid."

"Yeah, I know. But you could say that the team needs me—that it's not fair to them."

"I don't know." Coach scratched his head. "You know I want you on the team. We do need you. But what your Mom decides is none of my business."

"I've got it!" Stuart shouted. "Come to my house for dinner tonight—to help me with my math. I'll tell Mom I invited you—"

"Stuart," Coach interrupted. "I teach eighth-grade math. You're not even in my class."

"But I will be next year. And you can help me get a good start, and Mom's a great cook. You'll really like her."

"What?"

"I mean, she won't be mad or anything. She loves to have people for dinner. Especially if they're helping me with math. You don't even have to mention soccer."

If I can just get them both inside my house, Stuart thought excitedly, it'll work. I know it will! 401 Peach Street. It's not exactly the Empire State Building, but it'll do.

Coach looked confused. "I thought soccer was the

whole point." He narrowed his eyes at Stuart. "Is there something you're not telling me?"

"Nope," lied Stuart happily. "Look. She'll just be glad you're helping me with math. And that will make her feel guilty about messing up your team. Trust me."

"Isn't this all kind of underhanded?" asked Coach.

"Yeah," Stuart admitted, grinning. "A little."

Coach shook his head, shrugged his shoulders, and grunted a short little laugh. "The things I consider doing just to get a win."

"You'll do it?" Stuart exclaimed.

"No," said Coach. "I won't. But, believe me, I'd like to. Man," he groaned and pushed his hair back, "I'm sure your mom's a great cook, and I've got nothing to eat at home tonight except leftover soup. But I can't show up at your house uninvited."

"I'm inviting you," said Stuart.

"Right," said Coach, lowering his head and looking at Stuart from under his eyebrows. "Look. You ask your mom to come see me at school. Okay? And Stuart, I completely respect her decision, but I'd still like to talk to her. Maybe I could figure out some way to get you back on the team that she would agree with."

Stuart left the building feeling lower than dirt. Coach wouldn't come to Mom, and Mom wouldn't come to Coach.

Stuart wished Mack were around, asking him how he *felt*, so he could tell her, "Lower than dirt."

He scanned the school quad for her or one of her friends.

Did he really want to see her? Who knew?

He knew what dirt felt like, but he had no clue how he felt about Mack anymore. Or, even more important, how Mack felt about him. Lately, a bad, murky sensation in his gut had slogged its way up into his brain, telling him that Robert was dead onto something. Especially since pizza night at the Ellers.

Stuart couldn't help but notice that no one in Mack's family paid any attention to her that night—except Uncle Joe. Heck, she was practically the invisible woman.

And, when he thought even more about it, he realized that everyone in that house *always* zipped around in a million directions at once, barely noticing anybody else.

Stuart figured that could explain why she thought her uncle was so great. At the same time, he hoped it *didn't* explain why she was friends with him, a not-especially-clued-in seventh-grade guy.

As hard as he tried to talk himself out of it, Stuart couldn't help thinking that he was probably being used.

Was the only reason she hung out with him so that she could be in charge of somebody? Because he paid attention to everything she said? And no one else did? The thought made Stuart's chest ache.

It also made him mad.

Then again, weird as it seemed, he felt kind of sorry for her. She was cool. How could her whole family not notice? What if his mother didn't pay any attention to him?

"Hah!" Stuart snorted out loud.

He would give anything for his mother not to pay attention to him. Mack was lucky and didn't even know it.

Stuart slumped onto the grass near the school parking lot. He'd missed the regular bus home, so he'd have to wait for the activities bus—the one that everyone took after soccer practice—the practice he wouldn't be going to.

The whole team would ask him why he hadn't showed. Stuart groaned. He was so sick of being embarrassed by his mother's overactive parent genes.

He reached for his book bag so he could stretch out on the grass with his head on it. It wasn't there. Stuart felt around him, as though it might materialize out of nowhere. No book bag.

Geez, he thought. I must have left it in Coach's office.

Stuart started to get up and retrieve it, when another great idea hit him. Yes! He'd get Coach to bring it to his house. The wheels in Stuart's brain began to turn like a precision clock, all the little cogs clicking into place.

If he could get home before soccer practice was over, he'd call Coach's office and leave a message, begging him to drop Stuart's books off on his way home. He'd sound desperate . . . say something about needing them to study for a test . . . a huge test. One that counted for half of his grade.

Stuart grinned. By the time Coach got to his house, his mother would be home from work. Ready to fall in love. It would work! It had to.

But how would he get home in time to call Coach?

Stuart looked all around him. Maybe someone had a bicycle he could borrow. Two bikes leaned locked to the rack near the parking lot, but Stuart had no clue who owned them. Maybe he could call a cab. He emptied his pockets looking for money. A stick of gum, his house key, and a bunch of lint fell out.

Jordan's beat-up Honda pulled up in front of him.

"Hey, Wyrm," called Jordan, leaning over and rolling down the window. "Need a ride?"

"Yeah," said Stuart. "I do."

10

NOTHING LEFT TO LOSE

Either Stuart was stupid or he had a death wish—riding in Jordan's car for the second time in less than a week.

To make matters worse, Mack was in the car.

"Whazup, Wyrm?" said Jordan, cheerfully.

"Not much," answered Stuart. He muttered, "Hi," in Mack's direction.

Mack mumbled, "H'lo," then buried her face in her book bag, noisily rummaging through her papers.

Stuart wished the duct-taped seat would swallow him whole and spit him back out on the lawn at school. What had he been thinking?

He had jumped into the Honda on impulse, because he needed a ride—that's what. And he hadn't seen Mack until it was too late. Now, she was giving off major ice vibes.

And his mother was going to kill him.

And why? Because he was trying to help her—that's

why. She massively needed distractions in her life, and meeting Coach was the only way Stuart could think of to give her any.

She should thank him.

But in his gut, Stuart knew he was dead if she found out he'd ridden with Jordan again.

So? Now that he had a second to think about it, what else could she do to him? Any way he looked at it, he had nothing left to lose.

Oh sure, she could take away all his food, or cut off his toes, or chain him to the streetlight in front of their house and pour fire ants down his shirt, but come on. His mom was strict, not evil.

Besides, she couldn't keep finding out everything he did wrong. Sooner or later, with or without the Telepathic Parent Principle, he would have to get away with something. Maybe today would be his lucky day.

He began to get excited about his plan again. Should he tell Mack? She was still pawing through her book bag, ignoring him. What if she dissed his idea? What if she dissed him?

"You started *The Hobbit*?" asked Jordan.

"Not yet," said Stuart. "Thanks for the loan, though."

"Cool book," Jordan added. He glanced toward Mack, who was still poking around in her book bag. "Lose something?"

"Nope."

"You guys talk too much," Jordan joked, reaching forward and turning up the volume on the radio. He'd rigged some speakers that would blow your eardrums off.

The bass thumped in Stuart's chest and made him feel like a bongo drum. It was awesome. The whole car vibrated the rest of the way home.

"Thanks for the ride!" he shouted at Jordan as they pulled up in front of Stuart's house.

Jordan turned down the radio. "No problem."

Stuart climbed out of the car casually, in broad daylight, glancing around to see if any neighbors were looking. Or his mother. A weird, prickly combination of adrenaline and dread washed over him. Was this how it felt to rob a bank?

"Thanks again for the book," he said, trying to shut the car door quietly. It only half closed, so he had to open it again and slam it.

"See you," he said to Mack.

"No problem," she echoed Jordan, but her voice was sad.

Suddenly Stuart wanted to tell her he was sorry about the stupid stuff he'd said the other night, but that would feel dorky with Jordan sitting there. Besides, he needed to get out of sight. Now.

"I'm home!" he called, flinging open his front door and banging it into the foyer wall.

No answer.

Good. That meant Mom must be upstairs, in the back of the house, where she couldn't have seen, or heard, Jordan's car.

He bolted up the steps. "I'm home!" he called down the hall.

Still no answer.

He clattered back down the stairs and checked the carport. No car.

Had she forgotten that he didn't have soccer today? That he didn't have soccer ever? That seemed about as likely as some judge forgetting he'd sentenced a murderer.

Stuart's mom was at work by eight o'clock every morning, where she did paperwork until her store opened. That way she could be home around four—leaving one of her salespeople in charge—to be home at the same time as Stuart on the days he didn't have soccer.

He glanced around the kitchen for a note. No note.

Stuart Ellis would never be lucky enough to be a latchkey kid. Heck. He figured his mother would live in his dorm when he went to college.

So, where was she?

Stuart piled a handful of Triscuits onto a paper plate, covered them with grated cheddar, and popped the whole thing into the microwave. Then he called Coach's office and left a desperate message about his book bag.

He glanced at his watch. Soccer practice would be over in ten minutes. What if his mother wasn't home by the time Coach dropped off his books? What if Coach didn't check his messages?

While he was finishing his snack, worrying, and washing it down with apple juice, the phone rang.

"Stuart," said Mom before he could even say hello. "Sorry I'm late. We got swamped at the store, right at four o'clock. I'll be home in twenty minutes. Is everything okay?"

"Fine." He looked at his watch again. He did the math. His mother would be home in twenty minutes. If Coach went straight to his office right after practice, checked his messages, and then left, he couldn't get here in less than twenty-five minutes. Perfect.

"And Stuart, would you take two pork chops out of the freezer? We can have them with last night's leftover vegetables."

"Sure, Mom."

"Do it right now. Okay? You know how you forget."

"Okay, Mom. Right now."

"Bye, honey."

Click.

Stuart opened the freezer compartment above the refrigerator, hoping he'd find three pork chops, so that he could ask Coach to eat dinner with them. How could she say no with him standing right there?

Next to a white package marked, *Pork chops—2,* Stuart spotted a fat package covered with aluminum foil, labeled *Chicken, Rice, and Mushroom Casserole*. Perfect, he thought. Stuart removed it, shoved it in the microwave, and pushed the defrost button.

Krrrryck! Krrackle! Kryck-Kryck! Krrackle! A wild electrical storm raged in the microwave as baby lightning bolts sparked and flashed all over the place.

Stuart lunged for the Clear button. Then he pulled out the package, which now had a bunch of brown spots burned into the foil.

Geez, he thought, sniffing the burnt aluminum. He probably couldn't survive as a latchkey kid anyway. Even five-year-olds remembered not to put tinfoil in a microwave.

Stuart unwrapped the foil, placed the frozen casserole in a glass dish, and thrust it back in the microwave to defrost. Then he went into the den and stretched out on the sofa. The television remote lay on the coffee table, begging him to pick it up and click on the TV.

Why not? Stuart thought, picking it up. No, he reconsidered. She'll feel the TV to see if it's warm when she comes in. Even though there was nothing left to lose, he wasn't ready to morph into boy-rebel in just one day.

He sighed, picked up *The Hobbit*, turned to page one, and read, "In a hole in the ground there lived a hobbit."

Stuart became so involved in the story of Bilbo and his scary, unwanted quest, that he didn't hear his mom come home. Suddenly, she was standing in the doorway, look-ing puzzled and asking, "Stuart, why didn't you thaw the pork chops like I asked? There's a casserole in the microwave."

"I'm starved!" said Stuart enthusiastically.

"Oh . . . well . . . all right," she answered, then turned as the doorbell rang.

"Who could that be?" she wondered out loud.

Stuart turned a page, pretending to read, but his heart was pounding like an entire army of fleeing hobbit feet.

Mom opened the front door.

"Chris James," said Coach, extending his hand for her to shake. "Stuart's soccer coach."

James! thought Stuart, stunned. The *J* stands for James! No way.

His mother could end up being Jamie James!? How had he not known that? Had Mack known that?

"Of course," said Mom, looking confused.

"Is Stuart here? I have his books."

"Yes. Thank you." She hesitated, then took a step back. "Come in."

Yes! cheered the megaphone in Stuart's head.

Coach had on the short-sleeved knit shirt and khaki pants Stuart had seen him wearing earlier at school. His bare arms looked strong—muscular. Women liked that, didn't they?

He hoped Coach didn't stink too much from soccer practice.

"Hey, Coach!" Stuart called, closing his book and hopping up. "Thanks for bringing my books. I've got a test. You know. Social Studies. Big test." He prayed no one would check with Mrs. Franks, his teacher.

"You're welcome," said Coach. "Mrs. Ellis, you've got a great soccer player here."

"Jamie," said Mom, eyeing Stuart suspiciously. "Call me Jamie. And I know Stuart appreciates your bringing his books. I'm sorry he won't be able to play—"

"Coach," Stuart interrupted, "why don't you stay for dinner? We've got extra."

Mom flushed dark red, the color of dragon flames.

"Stuart," said Coach. "Thanks, buddy, but—"

"Come on, Mom. Ask him to stay. It's the least we can do since he drove all the way over here, majorly out of his way."

Stuart had no clue where Coach lived. It could be one street over, for all he knew.

Mom was dying to turn into Dragon Woman. Stuart could tell. But instead, she pulled herself together and said, politely, "I'm sure Chris's wife is expecting him home."

"He's not married," blurted Stuart.

That hung in the air like a tossed grenade until Stuart added, "Besides, he's got nothing at home to eat but slimy soup."

"Stuart!" exclaimed his mother. "That's rude!"

"No," said Coach, laughing awkwardly. "Actually, it's

true. But I don't want to impose. Stuart, I'll see you at school tomorrow." He turned to go.

"Chris," said Mom. "We do have a casserole. And I can make a salad. It's not much, but—"

"Cool!" said Stuart. "Mom's a great cook," he told Coach for the third time that day.

"Well," said Coach. "If you're sure—"

"She's sure."

"We'd love to have you," said Mom, forcing a smile. "But it's still way too early to eat. Would you and Stuart like to watch TV?"

On a weekday?! Stuart couldn't believe his ears. Having Coach around was working already.

"Let me get dessert," offered Coach. "I'll run to the store and pick up ice cream. What flavor sounds good?" he asked Stuart's mom, smiling warmly.

Stuart hoped she wouldn't say vanilla. Sometimes Mom lacked imagination.

"Well, I don't know," she answered, still looking like she was trying to decide whether to be warm and fuzzy or beastly and fire-breathing. "How about fudge ripple?"

"Fudge ripple it is," said Coach J.

"Stuart Ellis!" flamed Dragon Woman the second Coach closed the front door behind him. "If you think you and your coach can gang up on me and make me change my mind, you can forget it!"

"Mom," Stuart pleaded. "He's not here for that. We never even talked about it. I never even thought about it. Honest."

Stuart's mom sagged into a deep, soft armchair. "Do you expect me to believe that?"

No. Stuart didn't expect her to believe that. What did Mack say to do when he got caught in a lie?

"Say you're sorry. Then tell the truth," she'd said. "Fast. It works ninety-eight percent of the time."

"Okay," said Stuart. "I'm sorry. Maybe I did think about it. And maybe we even talked about it a little, but Coach wasn't interested." He eyed his mother to see if he had just tapped into forgiveness, or the two percent failure rate.

She watched him, cautiously, not saying a word.

Now what? Was there a third step Mack had forgotten to tell him?

"Mom," he plunged ahead. "I told Coach I had to quit soccer, and I told him why. Then, I begged him to come to dinner and talk you out of it."

Stuart watched his mother's jaw tighten.

"But he said no, that it was your decision and none of his business."

Her jaw relaxed.

"So why's he here?" she asked curtly.

"Because I forgot my book bag."

"And you expect me to believe that?"

"Yeah, Mom. I do. I forget stuff all the time. Remember?"

"I remember." She frowned. "And that's the truth?" she asked warily.

"Yes," Stuart confirmed. "I swear." Well, it *was* partly the truth.

"I'm guessing that's only partly the truth," said Mom, standing wearily and exhaling a soft little laugh. "But if he's gone out of his way to bring your books, and I've stolen his star player, the least we can do is feed him." She reached down and gave Stuart's shoulder a gentle squeeze.

"Thanks, Mom." Stuart's insides began silently and happily humming the theme song to *Sleepless in Seattle*.

"But, Stuart," she said in her period-end-of-discussion voice, "I'm not changing my mind."

For the next fifteen minutes, she banged around in the kitchen like a hammer. She pounded the casserole into pieces to help it thaw faster. She thumped three place settings onto the dining room table. She shouted at Stuart to take the stacks of magazines and newspapers that had collected by the back door and dump them in the recycling can. Next, she chopped nuts and peeled oranges for a salad, swirled up some fresh salad dressing in the blender, and whammed a bunch of knickknacks from one place to another as she dusted the tables in the den.

Exactly two minutes before Coach returned, she dashed upstairs.

"Are you sure this is all okay with your mom?" asked Coach, the second he walked in. "Was she mad?" he whispered.

Stuart was tempted to lie, but instead he confessed, "A little." Then quickly added, "But she got over it."

Stuart stuck the ice cream in the freezer, then did a double take as he noticed candles and Mom's good china on the dining room table.

When Stuart walked back into the den, Coach was sitting in a soft, cushioned armchair, straightening his pants legs, tucking his shirttail in, and looking generally uncomfortable. Stuart was used to the way Coach looked at practice—strong, calm, in control. Right now he looked as nervous as a kid taking a test he hadn't cracked a book for.

Stuart was beginning to feel a little the same way.

They sat silently, watching the soccer channel in the den that his mom had just dusted. When she reappeared, she had put on lipstick and a sweater that looked new.

Stuart thought she was going to a lot of trouble for a woman who didn't want to date anybody.

11

A GOOD THING OR A BAD THING?

Having Coach to dinner had seemed like an awesome idea—at the time. Now that it was actually happening, Stuart realized he would have had more fun watching reruns of *The Nightly Business Report* on PBS.

He had no clue how he was supposed to act while he was trying to hook up his mom with a man. He liked Coach—way better than Uncle Joe. But still, now that his mom and Coach were finally in the same room together, the whole idea of his mother with *any* guy seemed weird.

They sat in the den, feeling awkward and trying to talk about things that didn't involve soccer or how much trouble Stuart was in—which was hard. After all, soccer was the only thing Stuart and Coach had in common, and Stuart was the only thing Coach and Mom had in common.

"Don't you love this beautiful fall weather?" said Mom, crossing and uncrossing her ankles.

"It's great," Coach agreed, interlacing his fingers and putting them in his lap.

"All those leaves to rake, though."

"Yeah, I hate that part."

"Me, too," said Stuart.

They all smiled lamely at each other.

Stuart wondered if it would be rude to pick up his book and read. Why had he ever thought this would work?

He knew it had been eons since his mom had dated, but geez, they were both pitiful. He wished he had one of Mack's teen magazine articles to give them. Like "Twenty Tips for the Conversationally Hopeless."

After five painful minutes, Mom left Stuart and Coach in the den while she fled into the kitchen to toss the salad. The second she left the room, Stuart warned Coach, "She swears there is no way she'll change her mind."

"Well, we'll see," answered Coach.

Stuart privately thought that "we'll see" was an amazingly useless thing to say. No kid ever said "we'll see"—only grown-ups.

At dinner, they quizzed Stuart about school.

"Do you have much homework tonight?" his mom asked politely.

"Just an English assignment. I have to write a description."

"I thought you had a big test," said Coach.

"Oh, yeah." Stuart felt hot all over. The cover-your-butt details that went with lying were a pain to remember. "A huge test."

Mom nodded as if she knew all about it, even though she didn't. "Anything new in your classes?"

"Yeah," he said. "We're learning to use watercolors in art."

"What're you painting?" Coach asked, noticeably struggling to keep the conversation going.

"Waves at the beach. You know, right before a storm."

"I love the surf before a storm," said Stuart's mother.

"And the sky," agreed Coach.

Gradually, Coach and Mom discovered that they both loved everything about the beach.

"Pelican Dunes," recommended Coach. "Great fishing."

"My favorite is Solomon's Island," said Mom. "All those beautiful, old, weathered houses."

Stuart began to relax a little. It was a start.

Then they realized that they both loved biking. And reading biographies. Jamie began to talk enthusiastically with her hands. Coach relaxed back in his chair and laughed a lot. Stuart shut up and let it happen.

The next thing he knew, his mother jumped up and left the table to go look for *No Ordinary Time*, her favorite biography, so she could loan it to Coach. Coach got up just as abruptly and followed her.

Stuart sat, alone, still chewing chicken and rice, but no one seemed to notice.

When they hadn't returned after five minutes, Stuart, feeling smug, got up and cleared the table. He even scraped the dishes and stacked them in the dishwasher. Then he ate a bowl of ice cream by himself.

When he walked back into the den, Coach had relaxed on one end of the sofa with his arm extended across the back. He was saying, "if you like seafood, you'll love Scott's Grill. Maybe we could—"

Mom sat at the other end, her cheeks flushed pink, nodding.

"I'm going upstairs to study for my test," Stuart interrupted.

"Sure, honey," she answered, smiling at him.

"Thanks for the dinner invitation," said Coach, winking at Stuart, then returning his attention to Jamie. "They have the best tuna you ever ate—"

He *winked* at me? thought Stuart. What does that mean? That he just remembered he's here to get me back on the soccer team? Or that he's about to put some wicked moves on my mother?

Stuart climbed the stairs to his room, half of him hopeful, the other half wondering what he'd started— a good thing or a bad thing? Which reminded him of Mack. And how much he wanted to call her.

Instead, he picked up his spiral and lay down on his bed with his back against the pillows, his knees bent upward to support the notebook. He flipped it open to a blank page.

I'm supposed to write a description of a person, he thought. But who?

He printed *Mackenzie Eller* at the top of the page.

How had Mrs. McGuiness, his English teacher, instructed them to write the assignment? Oh, man, his shoulders sagged as he remembered—in blank verse.

The only thing blank was Stuart.

He chewed on his pen for a while, then wrote:

Dresses wacko, always rules. Picking friends, she favors fools.

He tore out the page, wadded it up, and threw it on the floor. Not only was it stupid, it wasn't blank verse.

He wrote *Chris James* on the next blank page, then crossed it out and replaced it with Coach J.

Coach J is a great coach.
How would he rate as a date?
Or a dad?

Stuart ripped out that page. Not blank verse, he thought, more like one of those Japanese Haiku poems. Mrs. McGuiness would think he was nuts.

What if his friends read it? They'd *know* he was nuts.

Stuart chewed on his pen, stared at the scabs on his knees, and thought some more. Finally, he wrote *Mom* at the top of a clean page.

When I look at Mom I see two people.
One smiles and ruffles my hair.
The other snoops,
stresses out,
makes rules,
breathes fire.
And now,
there are three of her.
The third's sitting downstairs
with Coach,
interesting, excited, talking with her hands.
Who does Coach see?
A girlfriend? A wife?
Does he see a mom?
Can he make a dragon disappear?

Stuart reread what he'd written, then tore out the page. Not only was it way too personal, he still wasn't sure if it was blank verse. Sometimes he hated English.

He wadded it up and pitched it across the room.

Then he turned over, propped himself up on his elbows, and opened *The Hobbit.* Maybe if he read for a while, it would jog his imagination and help him think of a subject for his poem that didn't televise his crummy life.

Would Mrs. McGuiness get mad if he wrote a description of a hobbit? What about a dragon?

So far, he hadn't come to very much about dragons,

but he was relating—big-time—to the hobbit that was the main character.

All Bilbo Baggins had ever wanted to do was hang around his hobbit hole, smoke a pipe, and "take tea" on time. Then who showed up in his front yard but Gandalf, a great wizard, bent on talking him into slaying a dragon.

Gandalf reminded Stuart of Mack—wise, and never taking no for an answer. And they both dressed funky.

All *Stuart* had ever wanted to do was mind his own business, play soccer, and master a few video games. But, no. Thanks to Mack, he was in the middle of slaying dragons and dealing with troll-like complications—like wondering if his closest friend was using him and whether he really wanted his mom to date *anybody*.

Stuart closed the book and rolled over onto his back. Come on, wasn't this what he'd wanted? Well, actually, it was what Mack wanted, but he had agreed to it. And it seemed to be working. Mom and Coach were hitting it off fine. If they started dating, she'd have a life besides Stuart.

Then *he* could have a life.

So why didn't he feel happier about it? Well, for one thing, it wasn't his plan—it was Mack's. Except for the part where he decided Coach could be the boyfriend instead of Uncle Joe.

And, as much as he hated to admit it, he wasn't used

to pulling this sort of thing off without Mack there to help him. One side of him wanted to call her up and shout, "Help!" The other side wanted to see it through, his way, without her. After all, she only liked him because he was her own personal, well-trained slave.

There. He'd thought it—what, deep down, he'dknown to be a fact ever since the day that Robert had suggested it.

Why else would someone like Mack waste time with somebody like him?

The phone rang, but he didn't bother to move.

"Stuart!" his mother called up the stairs. "It's for you."

Stuart stared at his watch. Ten after nine. And his mother was letting him answer the phone? Didn't she know it was ten whole minutes past his phone curfew?

Wow, thought Stuart, suddenly happy again. It is working. This time next week, I could be playing Flame Blaster and drinking Cokes with a girl in my room!

"Yo!" he said, picking up the phone in his mom's room.

"Stuart. Hey. It's Mack." She sounded hesitant.

"Mack! Do you know what time it is?" Stuart blurted excitedly.

"What? Oh. It's after nine. Sorry. Wait—" Mack's voice flipped from cautious to enthusiastic. "Your mom let you answer the phone!"

"Yeah," Stuart answered. "And Mack, you were right! It's working!"

"What's working?"

"Your idea. Guess who's here. Right now!"

"Uncle Joe!" she exclaimed.

Stuart's bubble popped. "No. . . . Look, Mack," he said apologetically. "I'm sorry about everything I said the other night. Your uncle's fine," he lied. "And you dress amazing. You look great—all the time. Okay?"

"Stuart." Mack sounded strange. "Who's at yourhouse?"

"Coach is here—"

"Stuart—"

"No, listen. Please. Coach came over to talk to Mom about maybe getting me back on the team somehow. But, instead, they started talking about the beach, and bikes, and books, and Mack . . . they hardly knew I was there. And Mom just let me answer the phone without looking at her watch."

"Oh." Mack sounded disappointed.

Which irritated Stuart.

"What?!" he demanded. "You think nobody's ideas are any good but yours?"

"Come on, Stuart," she said sadly. "Don't start that again."

"Look," he said. "I've figured some stuff out. I'm not your slave anymore. I know why you hang out with me."

"Because I like you?" she asked.

"No, because your family doesn't know you're alive."

The silence on the other end of the phone was so loud it hurt.

"What?" said Mack finally, so softly he could barely hear her.

Stuart knew he should shut up, but he couldn't. Everything that had been bugging him for days rose up inside him like a poison that he had to spew out.

"Your Uncle Joe and my mom are *not* 'the perfect pair.'" He practically spit. "You only want him around because he's a dork who pays attention to you . . . just like me."

"That's not true!" Mack shouted back. "Are you crazy? What's *wrong* with you?"

"Nothing," he answered firmly.

"I've got to go now," she said quietly.

"Fine," said Stuart.

Click.

Stuart held the phone, listening to the dial tone.

12

BODY ODOR BUS

When Stuart sat down in Mrs. McGuiness's last-period English class, he remembered that he didn't have a poem to turn in. The only two things he'd been able to think about since last night were, had Coach talked his mom into letting him play soccer? And why had he been so mean to Mack?

Even though it was true that her family didn't pay enough attention to her, he was sorry he'd said it.

He wasn't sorry that he'd said she only liked him because he was her slave, though. That was true, too. And he wanted her to know it.

Stuart ripped a sheet of paper out of his spiral and scribbled a poem to turn in.

Description — in Blank Verse
by Stuart Ellis

Mrs. McGuiness is a cool teacher.
I like her curly hair.

It frizzes on rainy days.

She drives an old gray car that's the color of buckets.

Stuart had no idea whether that was blank verse or not, but he passed it to the front anyway.

When school let out for the day, Stuart sprinted straight to Coach's office to ask him what had happened the night before. At breakfast, Stuart's mother had *not* said, "Honey, I've been too hard on you. You can play soccer again."

She also had not explained why two wineglasses were drying upside down on the drain board. Mom drinking wine!? On a Monday night? Was that a good thing or a bad thing?

Either way, if she and Coach had stayed up late, toasting Stuart's speedy return to the soccer team, she hadn't clued Stuart in on it.

"Stuart!" Coach seemed genuinely happy to see him. "Come in."

"What'd you and my mom talk about last night?" Stuart asked, noisily scraping a chair across the room and sitting down in front of Coach's desk.

Coach smiled. "Books, favorite beaches, the fastest place in town to get your oil changed, how hard it is to actually use frequent-flyer points, the best time to prune fig bushes—"

"Coach!" Stuart interrupted. "Did you talk about soccer?"

"Some."

"And?"

"Well"—Coach leaned back in his chair—"I talked a little bit about coaching. But mostly I told your mom how much fun I have with you guys."

"That's it?"

"Pretty much."

Stuart stared at Coach. There had to be more.

Coach leaned forward, placed his elbows on his desk, and propped his chin on top of his clasped fingers. "Stuart," he said earnestly, "your mom really does care about you."

"I know that," Stuart snapped, in a frustrated tone that implied *of course* he knew that. "But taking soccer away is stupid. Did you tell her that?"

"In a way."

"Really?! No kidding! You told her that?"

"Not exactly."

"*What* exactly?" said Stuart, growing impatient.

"Like I said," Coach paused and smiled. "I told her how much fun I have coaching—that I learn so much from you guys, and how maybe you might even learn a little bit from me, and a whole lot from each other."

Stuart thought about what Coach had just said. Then he grinned. Suddenly he understood exactly what Coach had done. He was letting Stuart's mom figure out her mistake all by herself—just like he did with his players.

"Coach," exclaimed Stuart, "you're a genius!"

Coach shrugged.

Stuart's irritation flipped to excitement. He knew his mother. "Becoming a better person—through sports." She would eat up every hokey-sounding word of it. Heck, she wouldn't want Stuart to miss another character-building second.

"Just keep telling her that stuff," he begged. "She'll add soccer to the list of things I *have* to do, like brushing my teeth, and homework—"

"You mean you won't care if I come over again some-time?" asked Coach, narrowing his eyes and giving his head a questioning tilt.

"Are you kidding!?"

"Stuart." Coach cleared his throat and twisted uncom-fortably in his chair. "I feel kind of strange about this—"

"You want to date my mom, right?"

Coach's face flushed red. "Yeah, Stuart, I guess I do. But not if that'll make things awkward for you at school. What if some of the guys on the team give you a hard time? I don't know . . . some people might think it's a bad idea."

Some people like Mack, thought Stuart.

"I think it's a great idea!"

"Really?" Coach laughed. "Now all I have to do is con-vince your mother."

Suddenly everything felt right to Stuart.

Besides, he was sick of flip-flopping back and forth. Did he want his mother to date? Yes. No. Maybe. Was

Mack a real friend or not? Yes. No. Maybe. All that inde-
cision was making his brain hurt.

He was ready to make up his mind. Yes. He wanted
his mother to go out with Coach. No. Mack was not his
friend. No maybes. Definitely no *we'll sees*.

"Stuart, don't expect miracles," Coach warned. "And
be patient."

Stuart was very patient. He was patient for the rest
of Tuesday. Also Wednesday, Thursday, Friday, and
Saturday. Every afternoon in his backyard, he practiced
shooting—volley shots, banana kicks, chip shots, headers.
With chalk, he drew a rectangle the size of a goal on the
side of the garage, and divided it into numbered squares.
Then he aimed the soccer ball, trying to hit each number
in succession. If he missed, he went back to number one
and started over.

Coach had come over three nights out of five, but Stuart
wasn't back on the team yet, and he was still grounded.

His mom was definitely distracted, though. He could
hear her and Coach talking so intently in the den that he
was positive he could boot up his Web site or play a video
game and she'd never know. Heck, he could probably
light bottle rockets in the hall.

She hadn't even found out that he'd ridden with
Jordan again. Stuart was so happy that he hadn't gotten
caught, he wanted to print bumper stickers and slap
them all over town:

STUART ELLIS BROKE A RULE AND DIDN'T GET
BUSTED! Finally!

He figured it was an omen. So he didn't want to take
any chances and get caught now. He was too close.

The problem was, he was bored. He could kick a soccer ball until it got dark, but then there was nothing else
to do. Zero. His mom was busy being flirty and chatty
with Coach. And even though Stuart had decided he was
fine with that, it didn't mean that he wanted to watch it.

He'd been grounded so long, all his friends had
stopped calling. At school, he'd told Robert and a couple
of the guys on the team that he wouldn't be at practice
anymore. They'd been bummed out for about two seconds, then gone back to making plans to hang out at
We've Got Game, or build a skateboard ramp, or rent
movies and spend the night at each other's houses. All
the things that Stuart had been cut off from.

He could always call *them*, but the truth was, he
didn't really think he had friends anymore. It had been
too long since he'd done anything with them. His mom
might think seeing them at school was enough, but she
didn't understand how things worked.

And Mack was definitely out. He hardly ever saw her
at school. And if he did, he ducked and went the other
way. He was about to get his life fixed, all by himself, and
what he didn't need was Mack telling him how much his
ideas stunk.

So mostly he read *The Hobbit* and waited patiently

for the miracle that Coach had told him not to expect.

It came on Sunday.

Stuart was hanging out at the breakfast table reading the funnies, while his mom leaned into the kitchen counter, dipping bread into egg batter to make French toast. As she dropped a slice of dripping bread onto the hot frying pan, the liquid popped and sizzled. At the same time, she said softly, "Honey, you can play soccer again."

Stuart wondered if he'd heard right. After all, the French toast was making a lot of noise. Maybe she'd said, "honey, you can never play soccer again," or even, "hurry, you can slay rock stars and win."

"Huh?" said Stuart.

His mother flipped the toast over. "I've been talking to Chris, and doing a lot of thinking." She watched the toast for a minute, then slid it out of the pan and onto a plate. She switched off the gas burner and sighed. "Maybe, sometimes, I'm too hard on you." Then she laughed. "Chris said half the kids your age do stuff I wouldn't believe . . . that compared to them, you're an angel."

Stuart stared at his mother, not sure whether he should agree or disagree.

"Anyway," she said, placing the plate of hot French toast down in front of him, "I think you should be playing soccer."

There were no competing French toast sounds. She had definitely said, "you should be playing soccer."

"You're lucky to have someone like Chris for a coach,"

she continued. "Besides, they need you, and that's made me feel like I'm punishing the whole team, not just you."

Excitement surged up inside Stuart. "Thanks, Mom." He grinned and reached for the syrup.

"And you've been so good all week, I think you can have your computer back."

"No more grounding?" Stuart asked hopefully.

"One more week," she said, smiling sympathetically and ruffling his hair.

Monday afternoon, Stuart sprinted onto the soccer field, eager to be back. He couldn't wait for Coach to see his improved soccer moves, the ones he'd worked on all week in his backyard.

"No way!" joked Robert, throwing his hands halfway up and moving back slowly, as if he'd seen a ghost. "Stuart Ellis, back from the dead."

A few guys slapped him on the back. All in all, everybody acted happy enough to see him, except maybe Jeff, who seemed too busy juggling the ball with his feet to notice.

"Stuart!" called Coach, strolling over and giving him a high five. "Glad you're back."

They scrimmaged for an hour. Stuart scored like a maniac. Nobody could stop him. His backyard practice had paid off, big-time.

Coach congratulated him and winked. "Ready for the game tomorrow?"

"You bet," wheezed Stuart, out of breath but excited.

Did that mean he'd get to play? The team rule was that no one could play in the next game if they missed practice without an excuse. Was being punished by your mother an excuse?

"How come he gets to play?" asked Jeff, pushing his backward orange cap farther away from his face.

"Why wouldn't he?" asked Coach, looking baffled.

"Because he missed practice all week. That's why."

Coach shot him a warning look. Coach might be laid back and cool, but you still had to show him respect.

"Stuart's absences are excused," said Coach firmly.

Jeff kept his mouth shut but kicked a piece out of the grass in front of him.

Coach turned and picked up his jacket off the bench. "I need two guys to round up the balls and take them back to the gym. Any takers?"

"I'll do it," volunteered Stuart.

"Me, too," said Robert.

"Stuart the suck-up," mumbled Jeff, just low enough that Coach couldn't hear him.

But Stuart heard.

"What?" he blurted, clenching his fists and taking a step toward Jeff.

Robert grabbed Stuart by his shirt and pulled him toward the empty field. "Come on, man. Let's go get the balls."

"What's with him?" grumbled Stuart.

"He played your position all week. I guess he figured he'd start tomorrow."

"Oh." Stuart could see why that would bug Jeff, but he didn't know why he had to be such a jerk about it.

Stuart and Robert hauled soccer balls and empty water bottles to the gym, dumped them in a box just inside the door, then raced for the activities bus in the parking lot. They hopped on, tried not to breathe too deeply, and headed for two empty seats in the back. "Body odor bus" would be a better name.

As Stuart made his way down the aisle, he heard someone gripe, "I guess I'd start, too, if my mother dated the coach."

Stuart whirled around, ready to confront Jeff, but Jeff wasn't there. *Brad* had said it.

Stuart flopped down beside Robert, his face burning.

"Brad's a dolt," Robert assured him. "Jeff, too."

"Yeah," Stuart muttered in agreement, but his head was spinning. How could anybody think he hadn't earned his starting position? He had *always* started—before his mother even met Coach.

And how did everyone know they were dating already?

"Did you know about Mom and Coach?" he asked Robert.

"Yeah, everybody knows."

"How?"

"Mack told some people at lunch."

"I haven't even seen Mack," said Stuart. "She knew Coach came over one night, but that's all."

"She saw his car," said Robert. "Every night this week."

"Nuh-unh," argued Stuart. "Not *every* night."

"You haven't seen Mack?" Robert asked, surprised.

Stuart suddenly felt proud. "No," he said smugly, "she's not running my life anymore."

"Are you crazy!?" exclaimed Robert.

"No way," said Stuart. "I just got smart. She's outta here."

"Out of where?"

"My life, you dummy."

"You're the dummy." Robert laughed derisively. "The hottest girl in eighth grade's your best friend, and you dump her? Are you nuts?"

"But you said—"

Stuart stopped in the middle of his sentence. Nothing made any sense. Not Jeff thinking he was a suck-up, or Brad slamming him, or Robert switching gears about Mack. Stuart turned and stared out of the bus window.

They're all wrong, he thought resentfully. Then he told himself that he didn't even care, over and over, as he watched about a million telephone poles slide by.

13

TERMINATOR TWO

Jeff, carrying an armload of soccer balls, ambled toward the playing field behind Coach. Who's the suck-up now? thought Stuart as he stretched his hamstrings to get ready for their game against Jackson.

Yesterday's insult still stung. I've *always* started, Stuart told himself for the ten thousandth time. He'd been saying that silently, again and again, ever since Brad had mouthed off on the bus. Did he honestly believe the only reason Stuart started was because his mother dated Coach?

Well, he'd show Brad. And Jeff.

Stuart smiled confidently, picturing his now-deadly banana kick, the one that he could make swerve around the goalie—right or left—into the net.

"Stuart!" hailed Coach. "How's your trigger foot?"

"Great," answered Stuart, thinking, please say something to the other guys, too.

"Mike!" shouted Coach, as if on cue. "You ready for the Terminator?"

"You better believe it," said Mike, looking mean and ready to spit nails.

The Jackson Tigers were undefeated, and "the Terminator" was what everyone called their star player because he always finished you off. If anybody on Stuart's team could stop him, it'd be Mike. He played sweeper, and getting past him was like dodging a moving wall.

Coach motioned everyone to circle around as he went over game strategy—which mostly was to pass a lot, shoot fast, and hope Mike could stop the Terminator dead in his tracks without getting carded.

Stuart couldn't wait. He felt lean and mean. A regular scoring machine.

Brad avoided eye contact with him, and Jeff slumped on the bench, in what clearly appeared to be a pout, but Stuart tried not to notice—or care. Hadn't he always started? Weren't his absences excused? Yes. Coach had said so.

For the first fifteen minutes, the play concentrated around midfield. No one on either side could get close to the goal, much less score. The Terminator went for the ball and missed, kicking Stuart and sending him sprawling into the dirt right in front of his own bench. A searing pain shot through his ankle. No call.

"You okay?" asked Coach.

Stuart had just leaned forward to peel back his sock and see if he was bleeding, when he spotted Jeff—eagerly hopping up, pitching his hat under the bench.

Stuart let go of his sock and gave Coach an I'm-okay thumbs-up.

Jeff kicked the dirt and sat back down.

Hurt ankle or no hurt ankle, Stuart was *not* coming out. He wanted to take off with the ball, dribbling the full length of the field all by himself. He'd show these guys.

Instead, he passed to Robert or Brad or whoever was open, just like he was supposed to. But the Tigers always tackled or intercepted and got it right back.

"Robert, Brad, Stuart!" called Coach from the sidelines. He signaled a crossover play.

Stuart knew exactly what Coach wanted—one of his forwards to position himself for a pass by running *toward* their halfbacks.

Noah, the Warriors' left halfback, took possession and dribbled the ball, keeping it on the right side of his body—away from the Tiger defender who was stuck to his left side like superglue. Stuart's ankle didn't even throb anymore. He ran toward Noah. Just as he passed him, Noah rolled the ball sideways toward Stuart. The Tiger defender ran ten more yards before he even knew the ball was gone.

At midfield, Stuart made a quick turn and dribbled back toward the Tiger goal. A defender moved in to cut him off. Stuart eyed Robert and slowed down, pretending he was going to kick it to Robert. As the Tiger halfback rushed in, throwing his leg forward to block the pass, Stuart dribbled around him, then took off—leaving him off balance and in the dust.

Stuart booted the ball to Robert, who kicked it to Brad. Brad back to Robert. Robert to Stuart. Quick. Crisp. Closing in on the goal. The Tiger sweeper stood directly between Stuart and the goal. Yes! thought Stuart. Banana kick. He struck the ball left of center, swerving the ball in an arc around the sweeper and into the net before the goalie ever saw it coming.

Goal!

Warriors, one! Tigers, zip!

Robert chest-bumped him. Noah pounded his back. Even Brad couldn't hold back a grin. The crowd cheered.

On the very next play, the Terminator took it all the way downfield, faked Mike out of his shorts, booted a sizzling low shot toward the left corner of the goal, and scored.

Warriors, one. Tigers, one.

"You went to sleep!" shouted Coach from the sidelines. He sent Jeff and two more subs in to give some of the starters a rest.

"Great shot," Coach told Stuart as he came off the field. "The rest of you guys need to defend first, celebrate later."

Coach examined Stuart's ankle, which was fine, except for the purple color.

Coach whistled appreciatively. "That's a first-rate bruise you've got. Let's hope you don't need X-rays."

No kidding, thought Stuart. Hospitals sent his mother over the edge, ever since his dad had failed to come out of one.

"It's fine. Really," Stuart assured him, wishing Coach would drop it. It didn't even hurt anymore.

For the next five minutes, Stuart watched as the ball stayed dangerously deep in Warrior territory. He was itching to go back in.

Mike executed two great blocks, which made Stuart, and the other guys on the bench, stomp their feet and chant, "Ancho Honcho! Ancho Honcho!"

Jason pulled off three spectacular diving saves.

Then, a Tiger wing lofted a high pass to the Terminator, who had his back to the goal. He jumped up, leaned back, and swung his foot way up in the air for a bicycle kick. He connected in midair, kicking the ball over his shoulder and into the goal as he fell onto his back, grinning like an idiot.

Warriors, one. Tigers, two.

Coach moved Jeff to Brad's position and put Stuart back in at left wing. They tried the crossover play again, but the Tigers were onto it. Nothing worked. Stuart broke open and called to Jeff for the pass, but Jeff kept it too long, and a defender stripped it away.

He must've heard me, thought Stuart. I *know* he saw me.

The blood rushed to his face. He wouldn't deliberately not pass me the ball! Would he?

At halftime, everyone chugged water, ate oranges delivered by Mike's mother, and spit seeds.

Coach J kept bugging him about his ankle, which was totally fine. Stuart wondered if Coach was showing extra concern just because he was dating Stuart's mother. He hoped the rest of the team wasn't thinking the same thing.

Twice, Stuart tried to get Jeff's attention, but he might as well have been invisible.

Right before the second half, Coach launched into a pep talk. "They're the best team in the league," he said decisively. "But we can beat them." He pumped his fist. "Mike and Jason—good defense. Stuart, I need you to shoot more. Jeff, try getting your passes off quicker. All of you guys, if you can't pass, change directions. Don't be afraid to run the wrong way if you have to. Then pass."

Stuart was pumped. If only they could keep the ball in Tiger territory, he knew he could get off some great shots. Another banana kick, a volley shot, a chip shot. He had them all down.

"And Robert, I'm switching you and Stuart this half. Stuart, you play striker—"

There was a just-audible collective intake of breath from the team.

"Striker!" Stuart couldn't believe it. Center forward! Robert played that position—always. He'd played it since second grade. Because he was the best shooter. Robert was *still* the best shooter. Wasn't he?

Stuart felt a bolt of adrenaline zoom through his

armpits and tingle all the way up to his ears. Was *he* a better scorer than Robert now?

"—Jeff, you go in at right wing—" Coach was still reeling off the assignments.

Stuart, excited and confident, looked around at his teammates. Brad, Jeff, and Noah were openly glaring at him. Robert stared blankly down at the grass, his jaw muscles pulsing like a heartbeat. Jason and Mike had already headed back onto the field.

"Go get 'em, guys!" shouted Coach.

Stuart sprinted onto the middle of the field. It felt weird being in the middle. Everything felt weird. He glanced at Robert to his left, then at Jeff on his right. Both of them faced forward, avoiding eye contact. Instead, they glared at the opposing Jackson Tigers as if they were pond scum about to be wiped off the planet.

Stuart felt terrific and so dead, both at the same time. He was center forward! But why was everyone mad at him? He had practiced, gotten better, been rewarded. He had earned it. Period. End of discussion.

Oh, man! He sounded like his mother.

Thweet! The ref blew the whistle to start the second half.

Forget it, Stuart told himself. Just play. He crouched, leaned forward, and tensed himself for the attack.

Coach told me to score!

The Warriors gained the first possession. Noah passed the ball to Robert, who took off downfield, dribbling.

"Robert!" called Stuart, finding himself open in the middle.

Robert passed it all the way across the field to Jeff, who had two defenders practically mugging him. They intercepted, and booted it half the distance of the field. For the next ten minutes, the Tigers kept the ball swirling around the Warriors' goal and Jason.

Mike rushed, tackled, blocked, and terrorized everyone in sight. Twice, he was called for tripping. The Terminator got called for pushing.

Nobody made the free kicks.

Jason caught high shots, low shots, blistering bullet-into-the-stomach shots. He dove right . . . and left. His shirt was muddy, his knees bloody.

Finally, Jason booted one of his saves all the way down the field. Stuart stopped the ball with his chest, maneuvered it around two defenders, and rushed toward the goal. He spotted Jeff open to his left and executed a quick side-foot pass. Jeff trapped the ball and got ready to shoot. As the Tiger's goalkeeper moved out to meet him, Jeff chipped it over his head—too hard. It soared over the net.

For a while, the Warriors managed to keep the ball in striking distance of the goal. Jeff missed two shots, one wide, one blocked, and Robert booted a low one that hit the goalpost but didn't go in. Stuart got himself in perfect scoring position four times, but Jeff and Robert never passed him the ball.

He couldn't believe it! They were going to lose the game because of some stupid grudge.

The ref called time-out for an injured Tiger defender. Coach motioned his forwards over to the sidelines.

"I don't know what's going on," he said, eyeballing Robert and Jeff, "but somebody needs to get the ball to Stuart."

Robert and Jeff nodded.

The hurt Tiger limped to his bench and the ref signaled for play to resume.

Stuart trotted back onto the field beside Robert and Jeff. "Guys," he pleaded, "I don't know what the big deal is, but we've got to win this game."

"Right," said Jeff, winking at Robert. "*We* will."

Robert laughed and shot Stuart a spiteful look that said, "in your face, dude."

The ball stayed at midfield forever, with both teams tangled up, trying to break free with it.

The Warriors were still behind by one.

Finally, Stuart intercepted a Tiger throw-in and he headed downfield with the ball. When a defender threatened him, he passed it to Jeff. Jeff passed it to Robert, who faked out a Tiger and moved toward the goal.

"Robert!" Stuart was wide open.

Robert shot straight into the sweeper, who blocked it.

Stuart felt rage boil up inside him. Time was running out.

The next time the ball ended up near midfield, Stuart

charged after it, gained control, and dribbled straight toward the goal. He faked out one attacker, then changed direction on another. He could be a terminator, too.

"Stuart!" he heard Robert call. "Over here!"

Stuart looked straight ahead, ignoring him. He dribbled it all the way downfield, no passes, no teammates. Just him, faking, screening, turning, flying. It felt great.

He got off a running shot that swerved around the sweeper and headed toward the left corner of the goal. As the goalie dove right to try and stop it, Stuart kept running. The ball hit the goalpost and shot up, back into play. Stuart headed it straight into the net.

The crowd roared. The Warriors cheered and jumped up and down. But no one pounded Stuart on the back. No one chest-bumped him.

He didn't care. Terminator Two had tied the score!

14

AWFUL, EVEN WORSE, AND WORSE STILL

The soccer game ended in disaster. It was awful enough that the Tigers nailed the game-winning goal with less than three minutes left on the clock. Even worse was the fact that everyone on the team acted as if Stuart were to blame.

He overheard Brad and Noah complaining, "Some striker! He hardly touched the ball."

Stuart wanted to shout, "I made the only two goals we got, you idiots!"

Couldn't they see that it was Robert and Jeff's fault for not using teamwork? A moron could see that. For cripes sake! They never passed him the ball!

Worse still, when it was all over, Coach congratulated Stuart, Mike, and Jason on a great game. To everyone else, he just said, "We've got a few things to work on."

"Way to go, Stuart," mimicked Jeff in a singsongy

tone, out of Coach's earshot. "I just luuuuved the way you hogged the ball all the way down the field."

All Robert muttered was, "See you around, Wyrm," as he tossed his jacket over his shoulder and strolled off toward the parking lot. But "Wyrm" didn't sound upbeat or friendly like he usually said it. It sounded more like, "Stuart—the stinking-crawl-on-your-belly-in-the-dirt scumbag."

This is so not fair! thought Stuart. What had he done? Nothing!

Okay, maybe he had hogged the ball at the end, but didn't he score? And what choice did he have? No one would pass him the ball!

And what was Coach thinking, anyway? Giving him Robert's position! He should have at least yelled at him for not passing! Didn't Coach know that everyone would think he was playing favorites? Wasn't he the one who saw trouble like this coming in the first place?

No. Actually that was Mack.

So, Mack had been right all along, thought Stuart, as he slogged across the quad to wait for his mom to pick him up.

"Stuart!" called Coach. "Want a ride home?"

Stuart winced and ignored him.

Some little kid called out, "Good game, Stuart! Tough loss."

At least everybody didn't hate him!

Mack. How would he face Mack? Should he tell her she was right? Apologize? Or just go through life and not have *any* friends?

How did he get into this mess, anyway? All he ever wanted to do was hang out with his friends, play video games and soccer. And get his mother off his back.

Was that asking so much?

Stuart kicked a rock and sent it skidding across the parking lot.

Apparently, it was.

Fortunately, when Stuart got in the car with his mom, she barely asked about his game. She was too busy chatting away about how good sales had been at work, and what she wanted to cook for dinner when Coach came over.

Stuart looked at her face. It didn't have that pinched look that he'd gotten used to. Mack had been right about her needing a boyfriend. Stuart had just picked the wrong one—for him.

He wondered if old-guy Uncle Joe might still be available.

When they arrived home, Stuart went straight to his room and booted up his computer. At least he had his game privileges back. He slipped Robert's Flame Blaster CD into his disc drive and watched it download. A soaring, scaly monster swooped onto the screen, belching flames.

Stuart shut off his computer. His heart wasn't in it.

Instead, he picked up *The Hobbit*, flopped back onto his bed, and began to read. Bilbo and his dwarf friends had finally reached the Lonely Mountain, where the dragon Smaug was fiercely guarding the treasure, but none of them could find the hidden door that would make it possible for them to sneak into his cave.

Ten minutes later, Stuart heard the doorbell ring, then the sound of Coach's voice greeting his mother.

The last person Stuart wanted to see right now was Coach J.

"Stuart!" Mom called. "Coach is here to see you."

No, thought Stuart, Coach is here to see *you*.

He pitched *The Hobbit* toward the foot of his bed, flipped onto his side, covered his head with his pillow, and pretended to be asleep. Someone climbed the stairs, hitting all the squeaky steps.

"Stuart," said Coach. "You awake?"

Stuart breathed deep and even, hoping it made him look as if he were catching major zzzzs. He waited for the sound of Coach's retreating footsteps . . . and waited . . . and waited.

Finally, he figured Coach must have split, and he just hadn't heard him. Stuart uncovered his head and rolled over.

"Good nap?" said Coach, grinning.

Cripes! thought Stuart. He's been taking snoop-and-sneak lessons from Mom.

"Okay if I come in?"

"Yeah," Stuart mumbled. "I guess."

"How's the ankle?"

"Fine!" snapped Stuart, too loud.

Coach crossed the room, stepping around Stuart's soccer cleats, dirty socks, backpack, and empty potato chip bags. He turned Stuart's desk chair around backward and straddled it, his arms folded across the rounded back, facing Stuart.

"What happened out there?" he asked with real concern.

"Out where?" said Stuart.

Coach shot him a cynical look.

"I don't know," answered Stuart, staring blankly at the ceiling.

Coach repeated the look.

Couldn't Coach leave him alone? Go flirt with his mom? Run out for ice cream again? Get more wine?

"Look," Coach said. "I'm sorry if my dating your mom has made the team give you a hard time."

"It's not that, exactly," said Stuart.

"What, then?" asked Coach, puzzled.

Man, thought Stuart. Here is Coach J, who can get other people to figure stuff out, and he can't see what *he's* done.

"They're teasing you. Right?" asked Coach.

"No," said Stuart. "They're hating me."

"Hating you!" cried Coach. "Why?"

"Because you're playing favorites," said Stuart.

Coach looked stunned. "Favorites?"

"You know, letting me play when I'd missed practice. Obsessing over my ankle. Putting me in as striker."

"I'd worry if any player got hurt," said Coach. "And as for playing striker, you earned that."

"I know. But it looks bad."

Coach blinked a couple of times. Then Stuart saw the lightbulb pop on in his head. "Yeah," he said, nodding thoughtfully. "I guess it does."

Coach looked so guilty and pitiful that Stuart felt sorry for him. Here was a guy who just wanted to teach math, coach kids, and maybe have a girlfriend.

And all Stuart wanted to do was have a few guys to hang out with, play video games and soccer, and not get busted every time he breathed wrong.

It had seemed so simple.

How had everything gotten so messed up?

"Coach," Stuart said, brightening as he got a killer idea. Duh! It *was* simple—at least the soccer part. "Just put me back in as left wing. Yell at me when I don't pass the ball. And don't freak if I get hurt."

Coach smiled, his eyes almost twinkling. He gazed proudly at Stuart. "You're a good kid," he said.

"Nah," said Stuart, trying to stifle a grin. "I'm a bad kid, remember? Grounded for life."

"I'm working on that," Coach whispered. Then he winked.

"Thanks, Coach," said Stuart. "You definitely psyched Mom into letting me back on the team. Keep hanging out with her and maybe I can even get unsgrounded."

A floor squeak made Stuart and Coach turn toward the open doorway. Mom stood there, a look of surprise and hurt turning her face into a pinched mess.

She turned and vanished.

"Jamie, wait—"

"Mom, no—"

They both heard the latch to Mom's bedroom door click solidly into place as she closed it.

"Oh, man," moaned Coach. "She thinks we've been plotting against her."

"No sweat," said Stuart, sounding more confident than he felt. "Go talk to her. You can explain everything. Mom's easy," he lied.

Stuart listened as Coach stood outside his mother's door.

"Jamie," he said. "Can I talk to you?"

The door opened and Stuart heard them both speaking quietly for a moment, then their footsteps retreated downstairs.

Stuart lay down at the top of the steps, his ear pressed between the railings of the banister, and listened. Vague murmurings drifted up the steps, then silence.

"Good-bye, Chris," said Mom firmly.

"But Jamie—"

The front door clicked decisively closed on Coach, cutting off the rest of his sentence.

Stuart wanted to throw up. Geez! As fast as he figured out how to fix one crisis, another catapulted into its place.

"Stuart!" Mom called.

Uh-oh.

Stuart rolled away from the railing so she wouldn't know he'd been listening, and sat up.

"Come down here!" shouted Mom.

Uh-oh again, thought Stuart.

Slowly, he lugged himself down the steps.

"Mom—" he started to explain.

"Don't even try," snapped Mom.

"We didn't—"

"Yes," said Mom. "You did."

"Look," said Stuart, talking quickly. "Maybe I did hope you and Coach would hit it off, and then you'd let me back on the team. But that was my idea. Not Coach's. Coach likes you," said Stuart. "I can tell."

"No," said Mom, sharply. "He likes you. He likes you on his team. And now that you're back on it, he won't have to see me anymore."

"Coach said that?!" asked Stuart, in disbelief.

"No," said Mom. "He didn't have to. I'm not stupid—"

"Yes, you are," Stuart interrupted.

Dragon Woman ignited like a match. "You watch it, Stuart Ellis!"

"I mean, no!" Stuart scrambled to recover. "You're not. Of course you're not stupid. But you're wrong, Mom. Coach likes you. He . . . he . . . thinks you're hot!"

"He said that?!" screeched Mom, blushing.

"No," said Stuart. What was he thinking? He could never say anything right. He didn't even understand kid dating yet. Grown-up dating was a major brain buster.

"Look—" Stuart pleaded.

"No, you look," said Mom. "You've meddled in something that's completely over your head. But it's done. Over. So there's no need to talk about it. Period—end of discussion."

Mom turned briskly and retreated up the steps to her room. Stuart heard her door shut with a sharp click. There sure had been a lot of doors closed in the last ten minutes.

Stuart dragged himself back up to his room and flopped onto his bed. Now what? he thought miserably.

He needed to talk to Mack. And he needed to talk to his mom some more . . . and Coach . . . and pretty much everybody on his soccer team.

"Man," he moaned out loud. He needed to talk to about a thousand people—who probably hated him—and try and explain to every one of them how everything had mysteriously ended up so totally wrong.

Stuart stared at *The Hobbit*, which was still lying where he'd pitched it right before he'd pretended to be asleep. Bilbo had finally discovered the secret tunnel that led into the depths of the dragon's cave. The fearful hobbit had also learned that not a single one of his dwarf friends would be venturing down it with him.

Just when Stuart had closed the book, Bilbo had slipped into the dark passageway alone, not having a clue what waited for him in the blackness.

Stuart knew exactly how he felt.

15

COSMO GIRL

Stuart's life was a wreck. He wanted to talk to Mack. Was that a good thing or a bad thing? Who knew? All he was certain of was that it *felt* like a decent idea.

He wished he could see Mack right that very second so she could ask him how he was *feeling*, and he could answer, "I feel like talking to you." For sure, that would have to be an awesome answer.

Should he call her?

No, he needed to see her. He wanted to watch her face focus and her eyes blink four times in a row while he listed all the goofball things that were reducing his life to rubble. Then he wanted to watch her gnaw on her fingernails while she thought of a way to fix everything.

But Stuart couldn't see her. He was still grounded.

So? Would Dragon Woman even know? She was shut up in her bedroom. Crying? Not likely. Breathing fire? More likely. Thinking up new ways to torture him now that Coach was out of her life? Definitely.

If only he could convince her that Coach J liked her for herself, not because she had a soccer-playing son.

Stuart stood up, squared his shoulders, and heaved out a long, slow breath. He was going to Mack's.

If he got caught, fine. He didn't care. He was probably about to lose all his privileges again anyway, for "meddling in something way over his head."

He tiptoed past his mother's closed door; inched down the steps, steering clear of the squeaky ones; and slipped silently out the front door. He knew it wasn't as dangerous as Bilbo going down a dragon tunnel, but it was scary enough.

While he stood on Mack's porch, waiting for her to answer the doorbell, he realized that he didn't have a clue what he wanted to say. Should he apologize and admit that she'd been right about Coach? Or just act like nothing had happened and beg for advice, the same way he always had, before he'd blasted her for using him.

Had she used him?

The door flew open.

"Stuuuuuuuey," sniveled Dillinger. "Where you been, little guy?"

"Around," muttered Stuart. "Is Mack here?"

Dillinger pointed up the stairway, then swaggered off—probably to pull the wings off flies.

He knocked timidly on Mack's door, still not knowing a single thing he planned to say.

"Stuart!" Mack cried when she saw him. Her face registered surprise, then, for a split second—pleasure. Unmistakable happiness. Stuart saw it clearly before she masked it with indifference.

Stuart's jaw dropped. Staring into Mack's room in disbelief, he completely forgot what he'd come there for.

"Wh-what happened to your room?" he stammered.

"Feng shui," she said, trying to sound aloof.

"*Fung schway?*" repeated Stuart, his mouth still hanging wide open. "Is that a disease? Are you sick?"

"No way." Mack laughed in spite of herself. "It's a lifestyle—ancient Chinese. I read about it in *Cosmo Girl.*"

Stuart stared at the totally changed room. *Cosmo Girl?* Was that a magazine—or an alien with a ray gun? All Mack's cool clutter had vanished. Poof! Gone. Vaporized.

Pale blue sheets covered her bed, and it had been moved to a new position in the room. No more *Star Wars* print. No aardvark pillow, no rock collection, no magazine stack, no collections of ants, skulls, or ostrich eggs. Even the awesome dragon tapestry was gone. In its place hung a large round picture of a waterfall, with lots of blues and greens in it. The desk, now facing the door instead of the window, had nothing on its surface except a nifty-looking black metal lamp beside a clear glass vase with green bamboo stalks sticking out of it.

Stuart was speechless.

It even had a different smell—fresh. Not the room deodorizer kind of fresh, but more like wet grass on a cool day.

"Feng shui," Mack repeated. "It means you get rid of all the clutter." She proudly waved her arms, encompassing the whole room, then quickly crossed her arms, trying to look casual again.

Stuart could see that she was dying to tell him about it, but that she wanted to stay mad, both at the same time.

"The right colors and furniture placement boost my energy—make it more positive," she continued, trying to keep her face deadpan, but a smile twitched at the corners of her mouth. Suddenly, she gave up. Her face almost glowed. "Can't you feel the balance? The flow?" she exclaimed.

"Huh?" said Stuart. He'd been thinking how cool it was that she didn't seem as angry anymore. Now, just when he'd started to get the hang of feeling things, she wanted him to feel *flow*.

"The blue and green and black," she continued eagerly, "is for knowledge energy." She hopped up onto her bed and sat cross-legged. "I kind of wanted yellow and white for creativity." She paused and blinked four times. "Maybe I'll do that next week."

"You're kidding, right?" said Stuart.

"No, listen, I'm serious. This stuff is really cool." Mack pointed to her desk. "See that? It faces the door now instead of the window. So I can see who's coming in. That's called a power position."

"Your desk is in a power position?" asked Stuart, still confused.

"Yep."

Stuart stared at the desk. It didn't seem particularly powerful to him. Empty now compared to what it used to have on it, he thought it looked pretty boring. Suddenly, he lunged into a kung fu position, one leg forward, one back, arms up and out.

"*Haaaaaah!*" he screamed at the desk.

Then he began to feint and kick his way across the room, chopping at the air with his arms, and yelling, "*Hah! Attack! Hah!* Power desk—prepare to meet thy doom!"

Mack fell off the bed laughing.

Stuart grinned and shouted, "*Hah!*" a couple of more times.

Mack kept laughing. Stuart kept goofing off—the way he used to. It felt great.

"This is *so* why I like you," said Mack, between hiccups of laughter.

Stuart froze, one arm up in the air ready to execute a karate chop. Huh? This is why she liked him?

Mack climbed back up onto her bed, crossed her legs again, and threw her arms wide. "Yep! This!" she repeated.

Stuart stared at her.

Mack smiled at him for a second, then got a serious look on her face and said, "Stuart, listen. I've thought a lot about what you said. You were right about my family. They don't pay any attention to me." She stared down at her bare toes and got quiet for a minute.

Stuart felt awful. He dropped his arms.

"I guess I've always known that," she continued, gazing back up at him, "but I never thought it could be causing me to latch onto people who *do* pay attention to me— like you and Uncle Joe."

Stuart felt his chest tighten, as if a huge hand were squeezing it. She was going to admit that she'd used him. Stuart the fool. He was sure his face looked all pinched and stupid—just like his mother's had.

"But I don't know," Mack said quietly, turning her palms up and out in bewilderment. "I honestly don't know. Maybe it *is* what attracted me at first. Who knows? But Stuart"—she paused and looked straight into his frozen face—"it's not why I kept on being your friend." She smiled abruptly. "You dummy—I hang out with you because you're funny, and because you don't go hormonally bonkers like all those guys who just want to hit on me."

Stuart realized he'd been holding his breath. He exhaled slowly. But he couldn't think of anything to say, so he grinned and said nothing.

"Friends?" said Mack.

"Friends," said Stuart. He was so relieved he wanted to high-five and chest-bump her, but that could easily be considered *hormonally bonkers*, so he didn't.

"As for Uncle Joe," Mack pumped the fire back into her voice, "he's cooler than you think. You just don't know him."

"Yeah," said Stuart, "I believe you." He was so unexpectedly relaxed and happy, he would have agreed to anything.

"So," asked Mack. "How's the boyfriend project going with your mom?"

Stuart groaned and flopped down in Mack's small upholstered armchair. At least it was one piece of furniture that was still in the same place. Did that mean it had power, or didn't have power? More energy, or less energy?

Stuart, for one, suddenly had no energy, so obviously, the chair wasn't helping him.

"You were right about Coach," Stuart admitted. Then, slowly and painfully, he explained everything that had happened to him in the last week.

Mack listened and chewed on her fingernails, just like he knew she would. When he'd finished, she sat, unmoving and silent. Then she blinked fast, four times, and announced, "I know exactly what you need to do."

"Recruit Uncle Joe?" asked Stuart tentatively, certain that that would be her answer to everything.

"No," said Mack.

"Dung fway?"

Mack made a face. "It's feng shui, dummy. And that might help, but it wasn't what I was thinking."

"What, then?"

"Do nothing."

"Do nothing?"

"Yeah," she explained. "The way I see it, most of your problems are fixed."

"No way."

"Think about it," said Mack. "You've already handled the friend problem. Coach knows not to do any more stuff that looks like he's playing favorites. Right?"

"Yeah. I guess."

"Besides, it doesn't sound like he's going to be dating your mom anymore anyway."

"For sure," Stuart agreed.

"So, Robert and the other guys will come back around."

Stuart nodded, then added, "Jeff won't."

"Jeff's a jerk. He doesn't count."

Stuart nodded again.

"We're friends again. Right?"

"Right."

"And thanks to Coach, your mom's lightening up. He's even got her believing you're a pretty good kid for a twelve-year-old."

"I *am* a pretty good kid," said Stuart.

"For a twelve-year-old," Mack added.

"Gee, thanks," said Stuart sarcastically.

"You're welcome." Mack smiled.

"So," said Mack. "Where's the problem? The friend mess is fixed—or will be. You've got your computer back, you're playing soccer, and you're not grounded."

"I am grounded," said Stuart.

"No, you're not," said Mack. "You're here. At my house. How can you be here if . . ." Mack stopped. "Stuart," she groaned. "Please tell me your mom knows you're here."

"Nope."

"You snuck out?"

"Yep."

"You are so busted."

Stuart forced a halfhearted smile. "Probably."

16

SO BUSTED

Walking back to his house, Stuart thought about everything Mack had said. Was his messed-up life really fixed? She'd made it sound possible.

Then why did he feel so rotten?

Because he was about to get busted again, that's why. It made Stuart's insides shrivel to think that he'd come so close to getting his life back, then trashed it all on a stupid impulse.

Well, not totally stupid. After all, he'd gotten Mack back as a friend.

Besides, who was to say he'd get busted? Maybe his mom didn't even know he'd left. Lately, he'd been lucky.

Cautiously, he opened his front door and peeked into the den. Empty. He glanced into the kitchen. No Mom.

Quietly and carefully, he tiptoed upstairs.

Ennnk. His foot struck a squeaky step.

Stuart stopped. He listened. Nothing.

He crept the rest of the way up the stairs. Halfway down the hall, he saw that his mother's bedroom door was still closed. Inwardly, he let out a whoop.

He'd made it! He'd actually made it! He wanted to run the rest of the way down the hall to his room, but instead, he continued to tiptoe, slowly, steadily closer to safety. He slipped quietly into his bedroom, closed the door, and slumped with his back against it.

All he wanted to do next was dive onto his bed, throw his pillow up in the air, and cheer. But he couldn't.

His mother was sitting on the bed.

"A dragon," she said, holding out a wrinkly piece of notebook paper. "You think I'm a dragon?"

"No!" Stuart shouted, immediately recognizing the poem he'd thrown away. What had he written? He couldn't remember. Something about his mom being two people. Or three. What else?

He didn't have a clue.

"Stuart," said Mom. Her voice sounded weird and kind of raspy. Not as if she were about to cry—but more as though she were struggling to keep Dragon Woman down. "Can you explain this to me?"

"It's a poem," said Stuart.

"I know it's a poem," answered Mom.

"I wrote it for English."

Mom took a deep breath. And then another one. Stuart was pretty sure that Dragon Woman was dying to break free, but Mom seemed determined to muscle her into a headlock.

"I want to know what you meant when you wrote it," explained Mom, slowly and patiently. "I'm asking you to tell me what you were feeling."

Oh no! thought Stuart. Not that!

He could tell her what he was feeling now—scared, stupid, and sick to his stomach. And wondering if she was going to kill him for going to Mack's.

But what had he been feeling when he wrote that poem? Who knew?

He remembered feeling that he hated English, but Stuart was pretty sure that if he said that, the dragon his mom had temporarily pinned would flare up, flapping wings so huge they would blow away everything in the room, including him.

"I don't know, Mom," said Stuart, staring helplessly at his mother. "Honest. I don't know what I felt. I can't even remember what I said."

Mom's eyes softened. "Honey," she said, "sit down." She patted a space on the bed beside her.

Honey? thought Stuart, sitting down. Did that mean he wasn't in trouble for going to Mack's house?

"Do you really think I snoop?" asked Mom.

Stuart looked at her in surprise. Do fish swim? he thought. He cut his eyes toward the poem she'd found—in his room—wadded up and thrown away.

"Oh . . . well. But Stuart . . . I just worry about . . .

never mind." Mom shifted her weight, cleared her throat, and started over. "Do you think I'm too hard on you?"

The blood drained from Stuart's face. Was he really supposed to tell the truth? What would Mack do?

Stupid, he told himself. Mack's not here. What would you do?

"Yeah, Mom," he said. "Sometimes you are."

"Is that why you invited Chris to dinner—to see if he could make the 'dragon' disappear?"

"Mom," said Stuart. "Can I see the poem? I can't remember what I said." Had he called her a snoop and a dragon? Apparently, he had.

Stuart's mother handed him the crumpled sheet. As Stuart read silently, the blood rushed back into his cheeks. He looked up at his mother, who seemed . . . what? Sad? Hurt? Mad? He couldn't tell.

"Stuart," said Mom, "do you want me to have a boyfriend?"

"Yeah. Kind of. I guess."

"Why?"

"So you'll be happy."

She looked superdoubtful. "And?"

"So you'll leave me alone."

For about an eternity, neither of them said another word. Stuart listened to the squirrels scampering up and down the tree outside his window. Playing? Gathering nuts?

Were they an omen? Which omen? That he'd be goof-

ing off with his friends again soon—or gathering food to
live on his own in the woods?

Finally, Stuart said, "I don't mean you should leave
me *completely* alone. But, Mom, you do kind of obsess."

"I need to think about all this," Mom replied in a
pinched voice.

"I try not to get in trouble, Mom. Honest. I try hard."

"I know you do."

"I'm not a bad kid."

"I know you're not."

"Am I in trouble for going to Mack's?" Stuart blurted.
He hadn't meant to bring that up, but he couldn't stand
it any longer. He had to know.

"So that's where you were," said Mom, nodding as
though she'd figured as much.

"I really needed to see her," Stuart said, gazing up
hopefully. "*Am* I in trouble?"

Mom sighed. "Yes, honey, you are."

"Oh." He wasn't surprised.

"If I stay grounded, I'll never have any friends,"
Stuart ventured.

"I know," said Mom, placing her hand gently on his
knee. "I've been thinking about that—a lot. So, I won't
ground you again. Chris has helped me to see some
things. . . . " Her voice trailed off.

"He likes you, Mom. A lot. He really—"

"Stuart!" she snapped. "That's enough. Don't involve
yourself in things you don't understand."

"But—"

"No, buts. Do your homework. I'll go heat up dinner."

Stuart's mom rose up like a storm and left the room.

Stuart stared after her. What did all that mean?

How much trouble was he in? He couldn't tell. If she didn't ground him, what would she do? Chain him to a streetlight and pour fire ants down his shirt after all?

No. She would never do anything like that. And not just because fire ants didn't live in his neighborhood, either, but because, Stuart knew, deep down, she was a good mom—and she knew he was a good kid. She ha   d said so.

Besides, hadn't he just had an amazingly honest talk with her? Not Dragon Woman. No. His mother—the one who pinned Dragon Woman to the mat and kept her there for fifteen minutes. Until the subject of Coach popped up.

Stuart wished things had worked out with Coach. But they hadn't, and he was tired of thinking about it.

He picked up *The Hobbit* and flopped back onto his bed. He'd left Bilbo in the dragon tunnel, and he had to get him out.

He read two whole pages before he realized that he couldn't remember a single word. He was still thinking about Mom and Coach. About how Coach had begun to make her realize she was too tough on Stuart. And about how the pinched look on her face had faded away when they talked about stupid stuff like pruning fig bushes.

Stuart slammed the book shut. His mother having a boyfriend was a good thing! Not just for Stuart, either. It was good for Mom.

Stuart wanted to fix it.

Don't involve yourself in things you don't understand, she'd warned.

But suddenly, Stuart did understand. Maybe not everything—like grown-ups dating, or drinking wine on Monday nights and having boring conversations about where to get your oil changed—but he understood the part that mattered.

Coach had stayed for dinner to convince Stuart's mom that he should play soccer, and because the food he had at home stunk. And *maybe that is what attracted him at first.* Weren't those Mack's words about Stuart— that maybe she started hanging out with him for the wrong reasons, but that's not why she kept on being his friend?

She became his friend because she liked him.

Just like Coach and Mom.

Stuart was sure of it.

All he had to do now was prove it.

17

HIT MAN

Stuart sat in his last-period English class and gazed out the window, past the parking lot, and over toward the soccer field. He couldn't wait for practice to start. Coach would put him back at the left wing position, and then he'd have a shot at getting his friends back.

After practice, he'd say something casual, like, "Anybody want to go to I've Got Game Friday night?"

They'd all gape at him and say, "You're kidding, right?"

That's when he'd announce that he, Stuart Ellis, was not grounded for the first time in forever.

At breakfast Mom had told him his new punishment—no telephone for a week. Big deal. He could IM his friends instead.

Dragon Woman was becoming extinct.

Stuart knew he had Coach to thank for that. He stared at the darkening sky. Too bad the Mom-Coach connection was becoming extinct, too.

He had lain awake for over an hour last night trying

to think of a way to fix it. Most of his ideas had seemed lame or completely crazy, but a few had the potential for total brilliance. Like tying his Mom to a chair and making her listen to Coach's declaration of big-time attraction, or giving them both anonymous tickets to New York City, with directions to the top of the Empire State Building enclosed. Once she got there, all those romantic vibes would turn her to mush.

Of course, when he woke up the next morning, those ideas seemed lamer and crazier than the ones he'd already rejected. Why did great late-night thoughts always seem stupid the next morning?

Stuart heard the distinct patter of raindrops.

Don't rain! he screamed silently though the window. Soccer practice would be called off.

"Stuart," said Mrs. McGuiness. "Your paper."

Mrs. McGuiness was standing directly over him, handing him back his poem. What had he written about? Oh, yeah. Her.

He unfolded the page and stared at the C she had penciled in red. She had written, "You can do better."

Stuart doubted it.

He watched the rain pelt the window, making clear streaks through the yellow fall pollen that had collected on the glass. Five minutes later, thick clouds and thunder still rumbled over the building. The intercom came on announcing the cancellation of all afternoon sports practices, except girls' tennis, which would meet in the gym.

Stuart ambled toward the bus. Now he'd have to wait another whole day to get his friends back.

Jordan's Honda pulled alongside him.

"Hey, Wyrm! Need a ride?"

"Nope," said Stuart. "Thanks, anyway."

He climbed onto the bus and sat in the first empty seat. He knew no one would sit next to him. Mack played tennis, and no one else liked him right now.

"Hey, Wyrm," said Robert. "Move over."

The way he'd said "Wyrm" sounded normal, like a friend thing, not scum.

Stuart slid toward the window and looked at Robert as he plopped down into the empty aisle seat. His spiky hair not only looked wet, it was wet.

"You want to practice soccer anyway?" he said. "I can come to your house, since you're grounded."

"I'm not grounded," said Stuart.

"No kidding?" Robert looked amazed. "Cool. You want to come to my house?"

"It's raining," said Stuart.

"Are you a wimp or what?"

"No, but—"

"Dude, I've got to work on my shots—so I can whip your sorry butt."

"Huh?" said Stuart.

Robert didn't answer. Instead, he fumbled around in his backpack and pulled out a bag of Butterfinger BBs. "Want some?"

"Coach is going to give you your position back," said Stuart. "You're better."

Robert pinched a few half-melted candy pieces out of the bag and popped them in his mouth. "Nope," he said. "Not anymore, dude. You're good."

"I don't even want to play striker," said Stuart. "I like left wing."

Robert ignored him and licked the chocolate off his fingers. "You want to practice or not?"

"Sure," said Stuart. Why not? Apparently Robert had decided not to be a jerk like Jeff. But the weird thing was that Stuart didn't want to play striker. At least not now. He didn't want to make any more trouble for himself.

He just wanted his old position back, along with his friends, and he wanted Mom to like Coach again.

"Coach isn't dating Mom anymore," said Stuart.

"Yeah?" Robert's tone was vague.

"I kind of wish he would."

"Yeah?" Robert sounded more interested.

"He got me ungrounded," Stuart announced proudly. He didn't want to sound like a girl, so he left out the part about his mom seeming happier.

"You better keep him around," Robert declared.

"I know," Stuart answered. "Somehow, I've got to get them both together, in the same room, so Coach can explain away this dumb misunderstanding they had."

"Grown-ups," said Robert, tossing back a huge handful of melted Butterfinger BBs.

"Yeah," agreed Stuart, wishing Robert would chew with his mouth closed.

For a while, neither of them said anything. They just sat and listened to the noisy bus full of kids.

"I've got it!" said Robert.

"What?" said Stuart.

"When the bus stops, you get off, then fall in front of it when it pulls away from the curb. While the ambulance is taking you to the emergency room, I'll call Coach and your mom. They'll both race to the hospital, and you've got it! Both of them in the same room."

"With me dying, you dolt."

"Just trying to help," said Robert, grinning.

"Thanks a lot," Stuart mumbled. But he wondered if it could work. Not getting run over by a bus, but just getting hurt a little bit. Definitely nothing big—hospitals freaked out his mom.

What if he got hurt at soccer practice and Coach and his mother both rushed onto the field to see if he was okay? Would that work? No. Mom wouldn't be at soccer practice.

She came to most of his games, though. When was the next one? Thursday. Two days away.

It could work.

+++

Stuart went to Robert's house to practice, then called his mom to tell her where he was.

It felt great—having a friend, being at his house, playing soccer in the rain. Maybe his mother was right. Matchmaking *was* way over his head. For a couple of hours, Stuart forgot about the whole Mom-Coach problem.

Later that night, Coach called his house three times, but each time Mom checked Caller ID and refused to answer. Stuart wished he could pick it up, but he couldn't—no phone privileges.

The next day, Stuart practiced at school with the team. He played great. Nothing showy, just solid. Robert was pretty awesome, too.

Coach was cool, didn't single him out, and only played him at left wing. Everyone on the team, except Jeff, acted normal. Robert and Noah made plans to go with him to the video arcade Friday night.

Guys are so easy, thought Stuart. How come moms and girls are hard?

The only time Coach even spoke to Stuart was after everyone had left. "You sure you don't want to play striker? Robert's looking strong, but you're every bit as good."

"Nope," answered Stuart. He loved left wing. It *felt* right. He wondered if that would be a good answer the next time Mack needed to know how he felt?

Coach nodded. Then he cleared his throat. "Were . . . uh . . . you and your Mom home last night?"

Stuart looked guiltily down at his scuffed cleats. "Yeah," he said softly.

"Is . . . uh . . . your phone out of order?" Coach asked.

Stuart dropped his head an inch lower. "No."

"I guess I figured that," muttered Coach, sounding kind of beat-up.

Stuart looked at him and knew—over his head or not—he had to think of a way to help Coach.

By Thursday, he had everything planned. Mom would come to his game. Stuart's team was playing the Preston Pirates, who had a defender so gigantic he made Ancho Honcho look like a pygmy.

Stuart was going to let him run over him. Not like a bus, but enough so that it looked like a major collision. Then Stuart would grab his ankle and act as though it were broken. Coach would carry him off the field. Mom would run to the sidelines. While Stuart groaned, Mom and Coach would bond over their shared distress. Stuart would recover slowly, then fake enough of a limp that, if he asked them to take him somewhere for ice cream after the game, they would.

He saw Mack at lunch. She was wearing hiking boots, jeans, and a floppy, wide-brimmed, khaki-colored hat. Should he tell her his plan? No, he decided.

After all, she'd advised him to "do nothing," and he didn't have time to fill her in on how he'd realized that his Mom still needed a guy in her life who was older than twelve. And how sorry he felt for Coach. He owed him.

After school, Stuart watched the Pirates scramble down the steps of their green activities bus. The second-to-last person off was number thirty-two, the monster kid Stuart had picked to deck him. He looked bigger than Stuart remembered, as if he'd been pumping iron.

Waiting for the whistle to start the game, Stuart was still watching number thirty-two. He hadn't been able to take his eyes off of him since he'd gotten off the bus. During warm-ups he heard the other Pirates call him Hit Man.

This wasn't baseball. Stuart was pretty sure "Hit Man" didn't refer to home runs.

Mom sat in the stands, looking down, probably so she wouldn't have to acknowledge Coach, who kept trying to catch her eye from the opposite side of the field. Beside her stood Mack, waving wildly to someone.

Uncle Joe!

What was he doing here?

Mack ran over, hugged her uncle, and led him by the arm back to her seat. Mom stood up and shook Uncle Joe's hand. Then they all sat down.

Was Mack setting up Mom and Uncle Joe again? Wasn't she the one who had said, "do nothing"?

Stuart stared at Mack, who was now waving excitedly at him. He decided she was probably just happy to be hanging out with her uncle. Stuart waved back, realizing he was glad that she had somebody to turn to.

Stuart shifted his focus back to Hit Man. His plan was to play most of the game before he faked getting hurt, but just looking at number thirty-two made him want to hurl.

The Pirates took control of the ball and started downfield. Stuart executed a sliding tackle, stripping the ball away and sending it rolling toward Robert. Robert booted it to Brad, and the three forwards took off, passing back and forth as they advanced on the Pirate goal.

Hit Man jockeyed for position in front of Stuart, who leaned left. When Hit Man lunged right to block him, Stuart shifted his weight, transferred the ball to his other foot, and swerved around the Pirates' monster sweeper.

"Over here!" shouted Robert.

Stuart whipped a side-foot pass straight to Robert, who sent it sizzling past the goalie and into the net.

Goal!

Warriors one. Pirates zip.

Everyone high-fived Robert, who immediately pointed at Stuart to credit him for the assist. Mom, Mack, and Uncle Joe whooped it up in the stands with the rest of the Warrior fans.

This will be easy, thought Stuart. Hit Man's big, but he's slow. He knew he could take him every time.

On the second possession, Brad faked out Hit Man and booted it high to Stuart, who headed it into the goal. Warriors Two. Pirates Zero. And they'd only played five minutes.

"Go Warriors!" screamed the fans. "Go Stuart!"

"Great teamwork!" cheered Coach. "Keep it up."

Jeff jumped off the bench, shouting louder than anyone.

Jeff's happy I scored? Stuart tilted his head, puzzled. Then it hit him. Jeff's happy because he knows Coach won't run up the score. He'll put in the subs.

Suddenly Stuart knew that if he was going to fake getting hurt, he'd better do it in the first half. If the score were eight-zip or something, Coach wouldn't even play him in the second half.

Hit Man lumbered menacingly at the other end of the field. Stuart took a pass from Robert and dribbled straight toward number thirty-two.

"Pass the ball!" shouted Coach.

Grudgingly, Stuart booted the ball back to Noah, who passed it forward to Brad.

As they neared the Pirates' goal, Stuart shouted, "I'm open!" Brad sent the ball toward Stuart, who trapped it and squared off against Hit Man.

You big blob! he thought. I could go around you so easy.

Instead, he gritted his teeth and ran straight toward the giant sweeper. He swerved slightly at the last second so he wouldn't be called for charging, trying to position his legs to tangle with Hit Man's. Then he could fall, gripping his ankle in phony pain. But Hit Man swerved, too, and their heads collided like two bowling balls.

Stuart felt a pulverizing pain above his right eye, saw yellow-white stars, and fell to the ground. He was only vaguely aware of a whistle, followed by a deathly silence. His head throbbed horribly, something wet covered his face, and he couldn't see. Suddenly, voices were swirling all around him.

"Time out!"

"I didn't mean to. He charged me."

"Stuart. Don't move."

"Stuart?"

"Geez. Look at all that blood."

"Off the field, boys."

"Somebody get a stretcher."

"Nooo!" screamed his mother.

18

SMELLY VIBES

Stuart felt himself lifted onto a stretcher and carried to the sidelines, where someone applied pressure to the right side of his head, just in front of his ear.

"He needs to go to the emergency room," advised Uncle Joe.

"No!" said Mom emphatically.

Someone put something cold on his head, then wiped away the blood.

"Easy," instructed Coach.

Stuart opened his eyes. Everything seemed blurry for a minute. Slowly his surroundings came into focus.

"Can you see?" asked Coach.

"Yeah," Stuart answered.

"Oh, honey," moaned Mom.

"Jamie," whispered Coach. "I think you'd better have someone take a look at this. Cleaned up, it's a small cut—probably won't even need stitches, but he could have a concussion."

Cool! thought Stuart. They're talking! If only it didn't hurt so bad.

"I'll take him in my car," said Uncle Joe.

"He's *not* going to the emergency room," said Mom.

"But, Jamie—"

"No!"

Stuart winced. Coach and Uncle Joe were both about to meet Dragon Woman. In the fire-breathing flesh.

Coach, Mom, and Uncle Joe moved away, but Stuart could hear them arguing while the school nurse gently put a bandage on his head.

Every third word, he heard his mother say, "No!"

The referee approached Coach, said something, then Coach walked back toward the player's bench.

Mom kept shaking her head emphatically at Uncle Joe.

"We won't leave him there," pleaded Uncle Joe. "You'll never have to leave his side."

The next thing Stuart knew, Uncle Joe and the nurse had loaded him into a strange car. Mom and Uncle Joe sat in the front seat. Mack parked herself in the back and gently patted Stuart's feet, which reached over and hung into her lap.

This wasn't the plan!

"Where's Coach?" he hissed at Mack.

"He has to finish the game," said Mack. "He'll come later."

"Come where?"

"To the hospital," said Mack.

Stuart couldn't believe he was actually going to a hospital. And that Uncle Joe seemed to be the strong, comforting, consoling guy who had convinced his mom to do it. *That* was supposed to have been Coach's job! Without the emergency room part.

"This isn't the plan," Stuart hissed at Mack again.

"What plan?"

"Shhhh," warned Mom. "Stuart, honey, you need to stay quiet."

For what seemed like an hour, Stuart waited. His mom talked to clerks and filled out papers. His head throbbed. Then someone in hospital scrubs wheeled him down a hall on a moving bed and tucked him into a cubby of a room with white plastic curtains for walls.

He wished Mack had been allowed to go with him so he could ask her what kind of feng shui a room with shower curtains had.

A tall, friendly doctor with a mustache held up three fingers and asked Stuart to count them. Then he asked a million other questions, while he shone little needle lights in his eyes. The whole time, his Mom sat two inches away, about to jump out of her skin.

Eventually, the doctor declared him whole, applied a butterfly bandage to the cut above his eye, and gave his mom a long list of symptoms to watch for. When they wheeled Stuart back into the discharge area, he saw Coach waiting nervously with Mack and Uncle Joe.

All three jumped up.

"Are you okay?" Coach wanted to know.

"Stitches?" asked Uncle Joe.

"You look funny," said Mack, who still had on her floppy khaki hat.

"I've got to get out of here," screeched Mom. "Now!"

Okay, thought Stuart. This is it. I need a plan B.

Whoa. Thinking hurt.

Too bad.

Somehow, he had to keep Coach and Mom together long enough for them to talk. But, right now, his original ice cream idea sounded like a piercing headache. And how would he get rid of Uncle Joe?

"Can I rent a movie?" asked Stuart.

"Of course," said Mom. "Joe, would you mind—"

"Not a bit," answered Joe, smiling.

Coach turned to go.

"Can I ride with Coach?" asked Stuart.

Mom stared blankly at Stuart.

"I'd love to take him to Blockbuster," said Coach. "Then bring him straight home."

"Mom," said Stuart, "ride with Coach and me. Please." He smiled at Uncle Joe and added, "to save you another trip out of your way."

Mom shot a dagger look in Stuart's direction.

Stuart smiled innocently and tried to look wounded—which wasn't hard.

Joe stuttered, "I . . . I don't mind."

Mack opened her eyes wide, then grinned at Stuart. He was certain she had just caught on to the plan.

"We'll all go," Mack suggested cheerfully. "Mrs. Ellis, I know you want to stay with Stuart. So I'll ride with Uncle Joe." She grabbed Uncle Joe by his arm and pulled him toward the sliding exit doors. "Meet you there!" she called over her shoulder.

Mom was stuck. Stuart knew it, and Mom knew it.

Coach winked at Stuart.

Coach knew it.

Nobody said very much on the way to Blockbuster. The tense vibes coming from Mom and Coach sitting in the front seat were so strong that Stuart could almost smell them.

Coach said the Warriors had won, eight to two. He'd played the whole bench, including Jeff, who had scored.

Stuart wondered if that would help shrink Jeff's jerkness, or make it worse. Who knew?

At Blockbuster, they all piled out of the two cars and into the store, even though Mom wanted Stuart to stay put.

"I'm fine," he insisted. "I want to pick out a movie."

"We'll help you look," said Mack, steering Stuart and Uncle Joe toward the section marked "ADVENTURE."

Coach knew opportunity when he saw it. He took Jamie firmly by the elbow and guided her down another aisle.

The last glance Stuart had of them was of Coach looking warm and genuine, but talking vigorously, while Mom actually appeared to be listening. On the shelf directly behind them, peeking through between their heads, sat *Sleepless in Seattle*.

Stuart was sure it was an omen.

"Have you ever watched this?" Uncle Joe pulled Stuart's attention away, holding up a video of *The Hobbit*.

Coincidence? Or had Mack coached her uncle on the way over? Either way, maybe Joe Eller wasn't such a bad guy after all. Hadn't he handled Dragon Woman and lived to tell about it?

"Cool," he answered. "I'm reading that right now."

Stuart was tempted to rent it, because he knew he wouldn't feel like reading again until his head stopped throbbing, and he was dying to find out what happened to Smaug, Bilbo, and the dwarves. He decided to wait, though.

While he and Mack continued to browse, Uncle Joe wandered off down another aisle.

A minute or two later, Mack said, "He really likes your mom."

"Yeah, I know," said Stuart. "Do you know if they got married, her name would be Jamie James?" He pretended to stick a finger down his throat and gag.

"Huh?" said Mack. "No, it wouldn't."

"Yes, it would. Coach's last name is James."

"Coach?" said Mack. "I was talking about Uncle Joe." She pointed across the aisle.

Stuart turned. Coach stood on one side of Mom, Uncle Joe on the other. She was flushed, but smiling, talking to them both.

Stuart stared.

"So," asked Mack. "How do you feel?"

"Not too bad," he answered. "Just a headache."

"No," said Mack, rolling her eyes. "I mean how do you feel about *that*?" She jerked her head in the direction of Coach, Uncle Joe, and Stuart's mom.

Stuart looked at his mom, who was talking excitedly with her hands, and at the two guys who were hitting on her. *Two* guys! How *did* he feel about that? Stuart tried to focus on it, but couldn't. He liked Coach better—and he hoped his mom did, too, but he was tired of grown-ups. Besides, it wasn't his problem anymore. He just wanted to hang out with his friends. Work on his Web site. Play soccer.

But Mack wanted an answer. How did he *feel?* Right that very minute? Suddenly Stuart knew. Headache or not, for once, he knew exactly how he felt.

"I *feel* like renting a movie," he said.

Mack groaned and hit him across the chest with her floppy hat.